Claiming His Runaway Bride

YVONNE LINDSAY

 MILLS & BOON®

First published in Great Britain 2009
Large Print edition 2009
Harlequin Mills & Boon Limited,
Eton House, 18-24 Paradise Road,
Richmond, Surrey TW9 1SR

© Dolce Vita Trust 2008

ISBN: 978 0 263 21002 6

Set in Times Roman 16¾ on 21 pt.
36-1009-44137

Harlequin Mills & Boon policy is to use papers that are natural, renewable and recyclable products and made from wood grown in sustainable forests. The logging and manufacturing process conform to the legal environmental regulations of the country of origin.

Printed and bound in Great Britain
by CPI Antony Rowe, Chippenham, Wiltshire

YVONNE LINDSAY

New Zealand born to Dutch immi-
grant parents, Yvonne Lindsay became an avid romance reader at the
age of thirteen. Now, married to
her blind date with two surprisingly amenable teenagers, she remains
a firm believer in the power of romance. Yvonne feels privileged to be
able to bring her readers the stories
of her heart. In her spare time, when
not writing, she can be found with
her nose firmly in a book, reliving
the power of love in all walks of life.
She can be contacted via her website,
www.yvonnelindsay.com

This one is for my beautiful girls,
Morgan and Tegan.
One day your prince/s will come…☺

One

His *wife?*

How could she have forgotten something like that?

Someone like him?

Belinda eyed the silent stranger standing beside her father at the foot of her hospital bed. Tall, and looking as if his designer clothes were just a little too large on his frame, the stranger stood with his left hand in his trouser pocket, his right hand resting on the knob of a shiny black cane.

She didn't even know his name. How could she be married to him and have no knowledge of it? Fear choked her throat.

His glittering green eyes never left her face. An intangible thread of something—was it anger?—burned just below the surface. His expression remained inscrutable. The hard lines of his face spoke of an iron will—this was not a man who tolerated fools.

Her breath hitched. She didn't know him— how could they expect her to go home with a total stranger? Belinda cast a frightened look at her father. The smile he returned seemed strained; the lines on his face deeper than usual. Suddenly her desire to be released from her room here at Auckland City Hospital fled, and the place she'd itched to be free of assumed proportions more in line with a much-sought-after sanctuary.

A disturbing thought occurred to her.

"If you're my husband why haven't you been here at my side, like my parents have? It's two weeks since I came out of the coma." Her challenge rang hollowly across the room.

Belinda intercepted a glance between her father and the man who claimed to be her husband, saw the imperceptible nod her father gave.

"Well?" she demanded, her hands fisting in the bedclothes.

"The accident that took your memory also caused me injury. I am fit to return home now. With you."

There was a great deal he wasn't saying, and what he left unsaid caused her more anxiety than the realisation he too had been hospitalised. She'd been treated with kid gloves by the medical staff and her parents since she'd regained consciousness, everyone prepared to give her medical answers but nothing else. Not even the details of the accident that had left her in a coma for four weeks. Throughout the past two weeks of tests and examinations, her doctors had tried to find the cause of her amnesia and had come to the conclusion it was not a direct result of the blow to her head that she'd sustained in a car accident. She'd overheard the words "traumatic amnesia" and "hysterical amnesia" being discussed in low tones.

The last had made her shudder. Did that make her crazy, she wondered, that she chose to forget a part of her life that for anyone should have been full of excitement, fun and passion? Or did she have good reason to want to forget?

She looked again at the stranger. The slightly less-than-perfect fit of his clothing now made sense if he had been stuck in hospital. Had he been too incapacitated to see her? Did a lengthy stay in bed explain his gauntness? She had no doubt that he was the type of man who paid attention to every detail, and that under normal circumstances his clothing would conform to his body as if tailor-made.

Another thought skittered through her mind.

Had they timed her release to coincide with his? Protest flared inside.

She'd been railroaded.

"No, I won't do it. I won't go home with you. I don't even know you!" Her voice sounded shrill, panicked.

The stranger's eyes narrowed, a muscle worked in the side of his jaw.

"I'm Luc Tanner, you are Belinda Tanner— my wife. Of course you'll come home with me." He nodded in her father's direction. "Do you think your father would allow you out of his sight if I was a threat to his precious child? Rest assured, you know me well."

There was an undercurrent in his tone she couldn't quite nail, but it was enough to send a shiver down her spine. She shook her head slightly to rid herself of the sensation. What the stranger—Luc, she corrected herself—said made sense but a cautionary niggle played at the back of her mind.

"Why can't I go home with Dad? At least until my memory returns." She was grasping at straws, and she knew it.

"And if your memory never returns? Are we to forever forget our marriage? Our vows to each other?"

There was a thread of steel in his tone that sent a chill through her. It was a good question. What if she didn't get her lost months back? And why, when she could remember so much else, could she remember nothing of their court-ship, their marriage? The love they'd suppos-edly shared.

A spear of something else shot through her body. Had they been intimate? They must have been, even now her body warmed to his with a physical recognition her mind refused to accept. He was a very attractive man despite that air of aloofness he wore like a warrior's mantle. A flush of heat suffused her cheeks as she studied his features—the slightly shadowed line between cheekbone and jaw bisected by a thin pink scar, the straight blade of his nose, the sensual curve of his lips. Had they lain together, delighted in each other's scents, reactions, pleasure? Had she clutched that short-cropped sable-coloured hair as she'd held him to her body?

The stranger's voice was like the sensual stroke of velvet across her skin as he changed tactics in the face of her refusal to go with him. "Belinda, I know you're afraid, but I'm your husband. If you can't trust me who can you trust? We will work through this," he cajoled gently. "And if your memory never returns, we will make new memories."

New memories. Why did the very thought strike dread into her heart?

She shot an imploring look at her father. "Dad?"

"You'll be fine, my sweet. Besides, you know your mother and I had planned to travel for a bit. We postponed the trip because of the accident. Now that you and Luc are well again we can set our plans back on track. Go home with Luc, honey. Everything will be all right."

Was it her imagination or were her father's words just a little too emphatic?

"The doctor has seen fit to discharge you. It's time for you to come home." Luc held out his left hand to her, a hand that bore a glint of gold on his ring finger. A ring she'd supposedly put on him while declaring her love for him before witnesses.

Belinda was suddenly aware of her own naked hand. There wasn't even so much as a dent in her skin to show where a ring had encircled her finger.

"Ah, yes, of course. Your rings." Luc slid his hand inside the breast pocket of his jacket and extracted two rings. He limped forward to the side of her bed. "Let me."

His fingers were surprisingly warm to the touch. They curled about her hand in a gentle, yet undeniably possessive grip. Something perverse inside her encouraged her to pull from his touch. As if he anticipated her action his fingers tightened as he helped her to her feet—his grip holding her hand captive.

He slid the platinum band, inlaid with baguette-cut white diamonds, onto her ring finger. As the overhead light caught the sparkle and fire in the stones, Belinda fought to control the tremor that quaked through her body, the sensation of having been branded Luc Tanner's property. A shocking sense of déjà vu swamped her as the image of Luc placing the ring on her finger in another time and place filled her mind. A remembered thrill of excitement and anticipation surged through her.

She fought to hold on to the impression, the fleeting consciousness of her lost months, but it dissipated as quickly as it had come, leaving her feeling empty and alone.

Belinda became aware of Luc's long fingers sliding another ring on her finger, bringing it up over her knuckle to nestle against the wedding band. The radiant-cut blue-grey diamond burned with cold fire, the shoulders of its setting decorated with smaller baguette-cut white diamonds. She gasped aloud at the size and beauty of the stone.

"Did…did I choose this?"

Luc's dark brows pulled together, making him appear even more formidable than before. "You don't remember this, either? For a moment I thought you did."

Somehow he'd sensed her flash of memory when he'd put on her wedding band. The implication of how well he understood her was unnerving, more unnerving perhaps than even the knowledge that she couldn't remember a single thing about him.

"No," she replied on a whisper. "I remember nothing."

"I commissioned the ring for you the day I met you."

"The day we met? But how...?" Belinda looked up at him in surprise.

Luc's gaze held hers. "I knew from that day you would be my wife."

Her laugh sounded forced, even to her ears. "And did I have any say in the matter?"

"Belinda." He pronounced each syllable of her name with care, making it sound like a caress. "You loved me before. You will love me again."

He lifted her hand to his lips, and pressed a kiss against her knuckles. His lips were surprisingly cool and an unexpected quiver of longing spread through her. What would it feel like if he kissed her? Would that unlock their past, the memories entrapped within her mind?

Luc drew her to his side, the imprint of his body heat seeped through her light clothing and deeper, to her skin. She pulled away, just enough to break the unnerving contact that had already sent her pulse into an erratic beat. His body felt unfamiliar, yet she was drawn to him at the same time. Surely if they had been married, been intimate together, she would have some physical memory imprinted in her psyche?

"The helicopter is waiting. We can't obstruct the hospital helipad for any longer than absolutely necessary."

"Helicopter? We aren't driving? Just how far are we going?"

"Tautara Estate is southeast of Lake Taupo. Perhaps being back there will assist in triggering a memory for you."

"Lake Taupo, but that's almost a four-hour drive from here. What if...?" Her voice trailed away helplessly. What if, indeed? There'd be no one there to help her if the fears that plagued the edge of her consciousness became more than she could bear.

"What if...?" Luc prompted, his lips a thin implacable line across his face.

"Nothing." Belinda dropped her head slightly, allowing the fullness of her hair to cover her face, to hide the sudden tears that stung her eyes. Everything inside her screamed that this was wrong, but she couldn't, for the life of her, remember why. The doctors had told her her memory should return in time, that she should stop trying to force things, but right now the black void in her mind threatened to overwhelm her.

"Then let's go."

Belinda walked two steps with Luc then halted, her sudden stop sending him slightly off balance. She noticed he used the cane to regain his stability. Was he fully recovered himself? She already sensed it was a question she couldn't ask, sensed he was too proud to admit to physical failure or weakness. Pulling from Luc's hold, she turned to her father, holding her arms out for a hug.

"I'll see you later, then, Dad. You'll give my love to Mum?" She searched his face once more for any inkling of why she felt as if she'd been shucked off like last year's haute couture, but he refused to fully meet her gaze. Instead he wrapped her in his arms and held her as if he'd never let her go.

"Yes, I will. She wasn't up to today's visit but we will see you soon," Baxter Wallace said, his voice thick.

"Baxter." Luc's voice cut through the air with the precision of fine steel, and her father's arms dropped to his side.

"Go on, darling, everything will be all right. Just wait and see," he urged.

"Of course everything will be all right. Why wouldn't it be?" Luc tucked Belinda's arm in the crook of his and guided her out the door.

Later, as the helicopter lifted from the pad, Belinda tried to remember why she'd been so excited when the doctor had told her she'd be discharged this afternoon. Now she felt anything but. She had nothing with her but the clothes on her back and the rings on her finger—rings that felt as foreign to her as the man who was her husband. She didn't even have so much as a pair of sunglasses to ward off the sharp late-summer-afternoon light.

She cast a glance forward to her husband who sat next to the pilot in the cockpit. Her husband. No matter what they said, he was a stranger, and deep in her heart she knew he'd remain that way for a long, long time.

You loved me before. You will love me again.

His words echoed in her mind and as they did it occurred to her he'd said nothing of his feelings for her. Not one word of love had passed his lips from the moment she'd set eyes on him. The realisation sat like a cold ball of lead in the pit of stomach.

Relief poured through Luc's aching bones as his Eurocopter Squirrel neared Tautara Estate—so named because of its position on the hilltop overlooking a small tributary river to New Zealand's largest lake. He consciously fought to stop himself from rubbing his hip to ease the ache of sitting in the confines of the cockpit of the helicopter. He'd accepted he was unable, at this time anyway, to pilot the craft himself. His recovery from the broken hip and torn spleen had taken longer than expected when a bone infection had delayed his rehabilitation.

The knowledge that his wife lay only a couple of floors away from him, locked in a coma that had baffled her doctors, had done much to hasten his recuperation. Her emergence from the coma had come just as he commenced intensive physical therapy and had begun to welcome the challenge of restoring his body to its customary strength. He'd had no desire to appear as a cripple the first time she saw him after the accident. He'd pushed himself hard this past fortnight, but it had been worth it. He was nearly home.

With her.

The chopper followed the path of one of the

lake's tributaries, where he often hosted trout fishing expeditions for his celebrity guests, and Luc took comfort in the familiar landscape, the energy of the land below reaching out to him. Yes, he'd heal more quickly here, in charge of his own progress. In charge of his life. The way it should be.

He cast a look backward to where Belinda sat staring out the side window. A fierce wave of possession swept through him. She was his. Lost memory or not, things would return to the way they should have been all along—before the accident.

Her misty blue-grey eyes were serious as she gazed at her surroundings, her face pale, her hands curled into tight fists in her lap. She'd barely moved for the duration of the flight. Frozen in the past he supposed. She didn't remember meeting him, their courtship or their wedding. She didn't remember the crash. A part of him hoped she never would.

As the helicopter gained height, then circled over Tautara Estate, Luc allowed a smile of satisfaction to play across his lips. The estate was a monument to his success and power and was renowned worldwide amongst the wealthy, the famous—even royalty—for its facilities and attractions. And it was home in a way he'd never had a home before. The words his father had beaten into him on a regular basis—"You'll never amount to anything. Nothing you have will stay yours."—echoed in his head.

"You were wrong, old man," he swore silently. "I *am* and I *have* everything you never were or ever had."

Yes, now they were back all would be well again.

The pilot set the chopper down on the designated pad and Luc disembarked, turning to help Belinda from the cabin. They walked in silence toward the main house, which sprawled before them. Belinda halted beside him.

"Is something wrong?" Luc asked, forcing himself not to scoop her up in his arms and carry her to the front door through his sheer will.

"I've been here before?" she asked, her voice tentative.

"Of course. Many times before our wedding."

"I should remember something, but I don't. There's…nothing there."

Luc sensed the frustration that held her in its grip and unbidden, felt a brief but undeniable pull of sympathy for her. The feeling left him as quickly as it had come.

"Come into the house, perhaps something there will jog your memory."

He took her hand in his and felt a measure of relief when her slender fingers curled around his, almost as if she was frightened to take the next step without him at her side. A grim smile settled on his face, and the fingers of his other hand gripped the head of his custom-made cane, its solid weight against the palm of his hand a reminder of the disability that would forever remain a legacy of their short marriage.

Whether she remembered again or not, he had her back at Tautara Lodge, where she belonged. As they crossed the threshold onto the New Zealand native parquet floor in the imposing cathedral-ceilinged entrance, Luc fought to hold back a roar of triumph. Nothing would interfere with his plans now.

No one reneged on Luc Tanner and got away with it—least of all his beautiful wife.

Two

Belinda stared around her. She felt as if she'd been totally displaced in her world. Nothing about the ornate stained-glass and rimu wood-framed doors at the front entrance felt familiar, and as her heels clicked on the highly polished wooden floor the faint echo rang out as a taunting reminder of the echoes in her mind. Fleeting. Intangible. Lost in a moment.

"Let me show you our suite."

"Our suite?"

"Yes, I run Tautara Estate as a luxury lodge

for overseas visitors. They pay handsomely for their privacy, I demand mine. Our rooms are to this side."

Luc led her through another set of panelled rimu doors and down a wide, high-ceilinged, carpeted corridor. To her left was a panel of floor-to-ceiling glass windows giving an exquisite view down through the valley, with Lake Taupo, sunlight glinting off its surface, far in the distance. The tranquil beauty of the scene lay in direct contrast to the nerves leaping and dancing in her stomach.

At the end of the corridor Luc swiped a key card and thrust open the door. Belinda stifled a gasp at the step-down lounge that spread before her. It was twice the size of her parents' formal sitting room at their palatial St. Helier's Bay home in Auckland. Twice the size and, by the looks of it, twice as expensively comfortable.

She walked down the stairs ahead of Luc. Her hand stroked the fronds of the potted palms that guarded the base of the shallow stairs and trailed over the surface of the baby grand piano nestled in an alcove of the room to her left.

"You play?" she asked.

Her fingers grazed the cool ivory of the keys, sending a single discordant note to hover on the air.

"After a fashion," Luc answered noncommittally.

Belinda lifted her head and met his gaze fully for the first time since they'd left the hospital.

"Did you play for me?"

Suddenly she needed to know. The piano was a beautiful instrument—an instrument of passion, capable of expressing deepest desires and yearnings even when words failed. As she waited for Luc's response his eyes changed, deepening in colour, becoming the stormy green of a storm-tossed lake. The scar across his cheek paled and she noted the tension in the set of his jaw.

"Luc?" she prompted.

"Yes. I played for you," he finally ground out.

The light in his eyes changed again, reflecting a heat that flared to unexpected life from deep within her body. She saw the muscles working in his throat, the twin spots of colour that marked the slant of his cheekbones— sensed the unleashed power of his body. Had he wooed her with music? Had she been seduced by the power of his long-fingered hands as they'd coaxed perfection from the keys of the baby grand? Had he then coaxed perfection from her?

A shiver of longing played down her spine, and she felt her breathing slow, her blood thicken languidly in her veins.

Belinda forced herself to break eye contact, to step further into the room with its luxurious fittings and deeply comfortable furnishings. Despite the value of each piece it was obviously a room that was used and enjoyed. Or at least it had been until they'd been hospitalised.

"I'll show you the rest of the suite." Luc's voice cut sharply across her thoughts.

"Yes, that's a good idea," she replied as she followed him up the shallow stairs on the other side of the lounge, to the informal dining area and small but functional kitchen. "So you're completely self-contained here," Belinda observed as they passed through to another corridor.

"We are."

Belinda couldn't help but notice his subtle emphasis on the word "we."

Luc continued. "The lodge has its own gym and indoor pool, and you can see the tennis court through there." He indicated a deep-set window that framed a vista out toward the back of the main section of the lodge where a full-size tennis court stood in readiness. "My office is located in the main section of the lodge."

"Do you have any guests here at the moment?"

"No. Not since the accident."

Belinda furrowed her brow in confusion. "Is it your off season or something? Couldn't your staff still have been able to provide their services and the full range of your facilities even while you were in hospital?"

"Certainly they could. I wouldn't employ them otherwise."

"Then why?"

"This time had been booked up for personal reasons."

She hesitated, noting how his hand had tightened on the head of his cane. His limp seemed more pronounced.

"Personal reasons?" she probed.

"Our honeymoon, to be precise."

He bit the words out as if they were poison past his lips and Belinda flinched at his tone.

Their honeymoon?

"Just how long have we been married?" Her voice shook as she asked the question.

"Not long."

"Luc? Tell me." Belinda pushed her back against the wall behind her, certain she'd need its support.

"Belinda, the doctors said you need time. You must take things slowly."

"How long have we been married?" she insisted, enunciating each word as clearly as she could through a mouth that felt as if it was stuffed with cotton wool.

"Just over six weeks."

"Six weeks? But then that means…" Her voice trailed away weakly. Her legs threatened to give way on her, and she braced her hands against the solid strength of the wall behind her.

"I shouldn't have told you."

Luc stepped toward her, but Belinda threw up one hand in protest as he leaned forward to touch her.

"No! Don't. I'm okay. I'll be okay. It was just…unexpected, that's all."

Six weeks? That meant they'd been involved

in the accident shortly after their wedding. But then why would no one give her any details about it? Why couldn't she remember?

Luc remained silent, his eyes flicking over her, searching for proof of her affirmation that she was indeed all right. He took a step away and turned to throw open double doors that led into a sumptuous bedroom. Her eyes were inexorably drawn to the king-size pedestal bed that dominated the room, dwarfing the exquisite outlook from the French doors that lined the outside wall.

Despite the generous proportions of the room and the bank of glass that allowed the crisp sunlight to warm the air, she felt the walls close in on her as the tension between them tautened like a drawn bow. Belinda could barely tear her eyes from the expanse of fine linen, the teals and blues of the damask duvet cover mirroring the tones and textures of the water in the far distance and the flora outside. She hadn't stopped to think about their arrangements once they arrived here. What if he expected to sleep with her?

An image imprinted in her mind of her body entwined with Luc's. Her throat dried, making it difficult to formulate her next words.

"Is this the only bedroom?"

"Yes. When we start our family we will extend this part of the lodge. I already have the plans drawn up."

"I would prefer to sleep somewhere else."

"Impossible."

"What?"

"You're my wife. You sleep with me."

"But—"

"Are you afraid of me, Belinda?"

Luc stepped close enough to her that she could smell the subtle tang of his cologne, the lime and spice intertwined into something that sent her pulse skittering through her veins. He lifted a hand to stroke a tendril of her hair back behind her ears. She tilted her head slightly, breaking the tenuous contact even as it began, but not soon enough to halt the heated tingle that danced across the surface of her skin.

"Afraid? No. Not at all," she lied. Afraid? She was terrified. As far as she was aware, their acquaintance, their *knowledge* of each other—be it physical or mental—had started from the moment he'd walked into her hospital room only a scant few hours ago.

"Then you think I would force my attention on you?" He cupped the back of her head, stroking her hair, forcing her to meet his gaze.

"I—I don't know," she stammered. "I don't know you."

"Ah, that's where you are wrong, my beautiful wife. You know me. Intimately."

With that he bent down. She was momentarily aware of the almost driven expression on his face before the distance between them closed and the coolness of his firm lips captured hers. She went rigid at the contact and felt his fingers tighten imperceptibly at the nape of her neck. Her lips parted on a gasp of shock and despite her determination not to return his caress she found herself unable to halt the answer of her body to his. The pressure of his kiss firmed, demanded more, and like an automaton she gave it.

She bunched her hands into fists to stop herself from lifting her arms, from curling them around his shoulders and pressing her body against his to ease the ache that made her breasts throb with need. Luc deepened the kiss, his tongue probing past her lips to gently stroke the soft inner recess of her mouth. A spear of desire drove through her from deep within her core. She fought the near overwhelming craving to be touched by him. To be dragged from the fugue of not knowing, to full aching awareness of Luc—of his taste, of his touch.

Abruptly Luc pulled away.

"See, we're not such strangers after all." His eyes glittered like chips of aventurine as he pinned her with his unblinking stare. Daring her to deny the way her body had awakened in response to his kiss. "There will be no force, I can assure you."

He limped toward the door, leaving Belinda standing there, alone.

"Where are you going?" she blurted. As unsettling as she found his presence, and her reaction to it, the prospect of being left alone was even more so. He was the only thing even vaguely familiar to her.

"Missing me already?" His lips fleetingly curved into an approximation of a smile. "I have business to attend to."

"Business? But surely it can wait. You must be tired. You're limping worse than before."

As soon as the words escaped her lips she knew she'd made a mistake. Luc Tanner was not the sort of man who liked to be reminded of his all-too-human frailty.

"Why, Belinda, you sound just like a concerned wife." He flashed her a smile that had nothing to do with humor. "My business has waited too long already. I suggest you rest until dinnertime."

He wheeled around on his good leg and left the room, leaning heavily on the cane she instinctively knew he had come to hate with all the seething passion she sensed beneath the cool surface he projected to the world. The seething passion he'd held in check while provoking a clamour in her that she knew already only he could answer.

Who was this man who was her husband? What had drawn her to him? And what on earth about her had drawn him in return?

She pressed shaking fingers against her lips. Had their attraction been purely physical? If her incendiary reaction to his kiss had been any indicator, she could certainly have believed that. But she'd never been overtly sexual. Her relationships had always been…civilised, for want of a better word. She had the feeling that any pretension to civilised behaviour from Luc was a mask. Beneath the surface, at grassroots level, he was indomitably feral.

So what was it, then? Had she been so drawn to the wildness in him, been so desperate to escape the confines of her "safe" world? She'd worked darned hard being the perfect hostess for her father in recent years, years in which her mother's health had steadily declined. She'd sublimated her own burgeoning career as a landscape designer, settling for the occasional showpiece job for her father's wealthy cronies. Jobs that had left her feeling as if she'd been appeased, like a fractious child. No matter how many magazines her gardens had been featured in, her family, including her two older sisters, had continued to condescendingly treat it as her little hobby.

Belinda sank down onto the comfortable two-seater couch, positioned to make the most of the expansive view across the valley. She knew everything about her life up until the point where she'd met him. Why couldn't she remember anything about that time?

Couldn't remember, or wouldn't?

The question chilled her to her bones.

She pushed herself up and out of the seat, determined to find something that would trigger a memory. He said she'd been here before, many times. Surely she'd left a piece of herself here. Something familiar.

She hesitated a moment before pulling open a door, almost fearful of what she would find behind it. It was one thing to want to know what had happened in the past, it was quite another to discover it.

A sigh of relief rushed past her lips as she viewed the luxuriously appointed bathroom. A massive spa bath lay along one glassed wall, a double vanity lined another, and set into an alcove was a large shower stall with multiple showerheads. Clearly, everything here was designed with two in mind.

She smiled as she identified her Chanel products in the shower stall, on the bathroom vanity. Her favourite fragrance and lotion nestled side by side as if they had done so forever. She reached out and grabbed the lotion, squeezing out a small blob and smoothing it over her bare arms, taking comfort in the familiarity of its scent.

Inside a drawer she recognised makeup and personal effects. All undeniably hers. Bit by bit the tension inside her started to ease away. As strange as Luc felt to her, this was her home. These were her things.

Emboldened by her discovery, Belinda went to investigate what lay behind the other door from their room. She laughed quietly. Already she was calling it theirs. It must be right.

A spacious dressing room with his and hers large wardrobes set on either side revealed an extensive array of clothing—for both of them. Formal wear, casual wear, in between. Belinda's fingers lingered over the array of fabrics and designs, hoping for a "ping" of memory. An image to hold on to.

A tremor ran through her as she reached for a garment, still shrouded in the cheap plastic dry cleaner's bag, and pulled it away from the rest. Even through the protective covering the myriad of crystal beads sparkled like tears embroidered against the cross-over bodice of the ivory satin bridal gown.

Belinda dragged the cover off. Her wedding dress. She should feel something, anything but this emptiness. Surely some sensation, some re-membrance should linger in her mind. She shook out the full train of the dress and held the gown to her and studied herself in the full-length mirror. She tried to imagine herself in it, walking toward Luc, ready to pledge her love and her life to him.

Nothing.

A frown furrowed her brow and she felt the beginnings of a headache start to pound. In frustration she haphazardly shoved the bag back over the dress and pushed the hanger back onto the rail. As she did so her hand caught on the dry cleaner's ticket, attached to the bag. She pulled it off and her stomach lurched as she saw the box that had been ticked for special attention—remove bloodstains—and the handwritten note saying the removal of stains was successful.

Blood. Had it been hers or Luc's?

She rubbed her forehead and gave a hard mental push through her mind, but all it elicited was a sharper edge to what had started as a dull pain behind her eyes. Whatever she'd locked in the past determinedly remained there.

It wasn't until she had gone through a few drawers of underwear and other clothing that she found a disreputable pair of jeans and a handful of T-shirts that, despite being laundered, were streaked with green stains. She sank to her knees as she pulled them from the drawer and unfolded them.

Her gardening gear. Her heart began to race. Finally she recognised something. Her hands shook as she kicked off her shoes and peeled away the clothes she'd worn home from the hospital—clothes her parents had brought up to her the night before—and stepped into the jeans. They fit. A little on the loose side, but that was only to be expected after her stay in hospital. She searched for a belt and put it through the loops, adjusting it a couple of notches tighter than the wear on the belt suggested was usual. A smile pulled at her lips as she pulled on one of the T-shirts. Yes, this felt right, and if she could get into the garden maybe she'd remember more.

Leaving her discarded clothing on the floor, Belinda slipped on a pair of rubber-soled flat shoes from the shoe rack and headed for the French doors across the bedroom. She flung them open, stepping out onto the private deck, and inhaled the herbaceous scents on the air.

Stairs led off the deck from the right-hand side, down into the impeccably landscaped gardens. As she danced down them, she cast her eyes around, waiting for that same spark of recognition that had struck when she'd found the gardening wear, but it continued to elude her.

The grounds were extensive and the sun was low in the sky when she found the herb garden. Crushed-shell pathways, edged with old bricks, formed a complex Celtic knot pattern, with lush foliage of a variety of herbs—their scents rich in the evening air—filling the spaces in between. At its central point a sundial was mounted, casting long shadows into the boxed rosemary nearby.

Rosemary—for remembrance. She'd have laughed out loud if the irony hadn't been so painful. Yet of all the places she'd explored in the garden this was the one area she felt most at home. Absently Belinda snapped off a sprig of rosemary and, rubbing it between her fingers, brought the fragrant herb to her nose and inhaled deeply.

Suddenly she knew. This was *her* garden. She'd planned and painstakingly directed the position of each plant in its place. The parsley she'd planted herself—she remembered that much—laughing at the time at something her sisters had said about how each time they'd planted parsley they'd fallen pregnant. The hope she'd felt that the old wives' tale would come true for her struck her square at her centre, and she staggered to the bench seat positioned to make the most of the final rays of the sun.

She remembered. Oh, God, she remembered the garden. It had taken months to get it to this state, but what of the rest? What of the time she must have spent here with Luc, of their growing relationship and their plans for a future together—their love?

The pounding behind her eyes changed in

tempo, sharpening to a vicious stab that made her flinch. As her eyes uncontrollably slid closed and Belinda began to lose her grip on consciousness, a question echoed in her head: was this the pain of remembrance or the pain of regret?

Three

Luc threw his Mont Blanc pen on his desk with scant regard to the limited-edition, eighteen-karat-gold masterpiece. He pushed his chair back from the desk. Damned if he could think straight today, and he knew whose fault that was.

Belinda.

A fierce sense of possession swirled deep inside him. He'd had to force himself to walk away from her earlier, to give her space, when all he'd wanted to do was imprint himself back into her mind, her body. He could have done it. She'd welcomed his kiss, participated fully in the duel of senses. But some perverse sense of honour embedded in his psyche insisted she come to him again willingly.

He pushed himself up and out of his chair and crossed his expansive office to the window overlooking the gardens. His first thought on seeing the young woman in tattered jeans and a T-shirt was that they had a trespasser on the property, but the quickening inside him told him exactly who it was. He'd had the same visceral reaction the first time he'd laid eyes on her and decided she'd be his. He smiled.

Expanding the existing kitchen garden had been the impetus to orchestrate her arrival at Tautara Estate. He'd done his research and known she would never be able to resist the opportunity to create an herb garden to rival any other in the country. Didier, the chef he'd unabashedly poached from a Côte D'Azur five-star hotel, had long bemoaned the lack of an extensive array of fresh herbs to use in his sumptuous cuisine and had theatrically fallen to the ground to kiss Belinda's feet once the garden had been planted.

Her lengthy stay at Tautara, punctuated by trips back to Auckland to act as hostess for her father's enumerable functions, had set the scene for his successful campaign. She had been away often enough to miss him—enough to realise she loved him and belonged here, at his side. It had taken time, but he'd achieved his goal.

But then Luc Tanner was the kind of man who always got what he wanted and he'd wanted Belinda with a gut-deep need that surpassed anything he'd known before. He thought back to the first time he'd seen Belinda, at a boutique hoteliers' function hosted by her father.

Rather than approach her directly, Luc had gone instead to her father, Baxter Wallace, who'd laughed in Luc's face at his request for an introduction to his precious youngest daughter and turned him down flat. Undeterred, Luc had bided his time, always watching from afar, knowing, eventually, he would succeed in his quest. And the time came, as it always did.

When, several months later, Baxter was fleeced to the tune of several hundreds of thousands of dollars in a credit-card scam targeting boutique hotels and chains, his bank had happily entered into extensive loans to rectify the situation. But by the time Baxter's wife had been diagnosed with a rare form of cancer, requiring expensive treatment overseas not covered by their insurance company, the banks had already capped their financial well. So to whom had a desperate Baxter turned?

Luc Tanner.

No one else had the resources, or the motivation, to help. And much as it had obviously galled Baxter Wallace to turn to the one man he'd spurned, he'd succumbed in the end.

They'd come to an agreement, one that had

suited them both. One that now hung on whether or not Belinda regained her memory.

Luc's eyes narrowed as he saw Belinda drop to the surface of a bench seat in the garden, one hand pressed to her head. Something was very wrong. He propelled himself toward the door, calling to Manu, his majordomo, for assistance even as she slid to the ground.

Manu reached her first. Luc's hand ached from his grip on the head of his walking cane and he silently and vehemently cursed the disability that had prevented him from being at his wife's side when she needed him.

"What do you think? Is she okay?" Luc asked, as the one man he trusted above all others checked Belinda's vital signs.

"She's coming round, it's just a faint, I reckon."

Luc clumsily dropped to his knees, ignoring the shaft of pain that speared through his hip, and brushed the hair from Belinda's face just as her eyes fluttered open.

"Luc?" Her voice was weak, her eyes unfocused.

"You fainted. Manu's checking you over to make sure you haven't hurt yourself. Don't worry. I trust him with my life."

"She looks fine, Luc. No sign of any bumps on her head. No grazes anywhere."

"How do you feel?" Luc wrapped his arm around Belinda's shoulders as she struggled to sit up.

"I…I don't know what happened. One minute I was okay, with a bit of a headache, the next it was excruciating pain. Then you guys were here."

"And now? The headache. Has it gone?" As soon as he had her back inside the house he would call her neurologist. He didn't like the sound of this headache. Not if it had the capacity to render her unconscious.

"It's going away. I'll be fine in a minute."

Her pale face belied her words. Between them, the two men helped Belinda to her feet.

Luc felt frustrated that he had to defer to Manu's unencumbered strength in this situation. Before the accident he would simply have lifted Belinda into his arms and carried her to their suite, but now even such a responsibility was denied him. They walked slowly to the lower entry to the house where an elevator door stood open and waiting. It was a short ride to the next level, where they made their way to Luc and Belinda's private suite.

"I'll arrange for your evening meal to be sent through to you," Manu said as he left them at the door to their rooms.

"Thank you—" Luc clasped his seneschal's hand "—for everything."

"Not a problem, Luc. You know I'm here for you, man."

Luc gave a sharp, brief nod. He and Manu went back further than either of them wanted to admit. The bond they'd formed in their preteens, occasionally tripping on the wrong side of the law in a vain attempt to shake off their respective parents' unsavoury influence, was immutable.

Belinda dropped into one of the deep leather couches in the sunken living room with an audible sigh.

"I'm calling your doctor." Luc crossed the room and lifted a cordless handset from a side table. He punched in the private number of her specialist without once referring to the card the man had given him prior to Belinda's release from hospital.

"No, please. Don't. I'll be okay. I probably just overdid things is all. I was trying to force myself to remember. Doing everything I'd been told not to do." She rose and took the phone from him, firmly replacing it on its station. "Honestly, I'll be fine."

"You will tell me immediately if you suffer another of these headaches," he insisted.

"Yes, of course." Her eyes briefly met his before fluttering away.

Would she? Her body language told him differently, but he had to give her the benefit of the doubt.

"Until I'm satisfied you won't have a recurrence of today's episode I don't want you out of my sight." It was a vow as much as a statement, and he saw her stiffen at his words.

"Surely that won't be necessary, besides being totally impractical," she argued gently.

"Let me be the judge of that. I will at least need to know where you are at all times." He took her hand and drew her toward him, placing her hand over his heart. The air between them heated with the warmth of their bodies. "I nearly lost you once already. I'm not prepared to take any more chances."

He saw the shiver run down her spine, the flare of her nostrils, the widening of her eyes as the impact of his words sank in. On the surface he knew they appeared to be little more than what one would expect from a newly wed groom to his bride. Only he knew the difference.

Belinda allowed his words to penetrate into the dark recesses of her mind. She should feel comforted, reassured by his protectiveness, but instead she felt only trepidation. He still held her hand against his chest, and she tried not to focus on the strong, steady beat of his heart, the breadth of muscle she felt beneath her fingertips.

Or the overwhelming desire she had to flex her hand against his strength, to imprint the shape and feel of him against her palm. Her heart picked up a beat and skittered in her chest as her eyes met his.

His gaze was unbreakable, and she was drawn even closer to him as she returned his stare. Now there was no air between them, her body was against his, length to length. Had he pulled her closer, or had she crossed that final barrier of distance without realising it herself? The long, strong muscles of his thighs pressed against hers, her pelvis cradled his slightly narrower hips, the soft curve of her belly moulded against the washboard hardness of his.

His pupils dilated and she felt his indrawn breath as if it had come from deep inside her own chest. Maybe it had. Already the lines between where she began and ended were blurred as she parted her lips, moistening their suddenly dry surface with the tip of her tongue. His own lips were set in a firm line, his brows drawn together slightly.

"Luc?" Her voice broke from her throat as more of a plea than a reassurance, and she felt the tension in him break as he lowered his head and caught her lips in a kiss that threatened to knock her hard-fought equilibrium six ways from Sunday.

If anything she felt more light-headed than she had in the garden when she'd regained consciousness, yet something still held her back, prevented her from committing fully to his touch. She drew back, feeling the loss of him like a physical ache as he let go her hand and she no longer absorbed his heartbeat or his heat.

He turned away from her and tunnelled one hand through his short-cropped hair in a gesture that told her more than any of his carefully calculated words. So, her cool, calm and collected husband could be rattled. Somehow the knowledge didn't give her the power she had hoped.

"I'm going to shower before our dinner arrives. Join me."

His invitation—or was it more of a command?—hung on the air between them as he limped up the shallow stairs toward their bedroom, his cane stabbing at the thickly carpeted surface like some kind of weapon.

Belinda's throat constricted on her words of denial. They were husband and wife, no matter how foreign the words felt to her. Dare she bare herself to a man who was essentially unknown to her? Would she find familiarity in his touch?

She took a tentative step toward him, then halted as fear overtook her need for the truth.

"Belinda. I meant what I said about you not being out of my sight." Luc paused at the top of the stairs, his body vibrating with a tension that was almost palpable. "You don't need to shower with me if it makes you uncomfortable, but I want you there. In the room with me."

A thrill of something charged through her veins. Was this a test of some sort?

"Fine," she answered unsteadily. "But I think I'd rather have a bath."

"I'll draw it for you."

"I can manage myself."

"Of course you can." His voice was conciliatory. "But let me do this for you. For my wife. I've been able to do little else for you in the past six weeks."

She sensed a hidden message in his last words and it left a prickle of discomfort running across her scalp. She shook her head lightly to rid herself of the sensation. She was being overly sensitive. Not surprising really when only this morning she'd been safely ensconced in a private room in hospital. Suddenly she couldn't wait to immerse herself in clean, soft water, to rid herself of the remnants of any lingering scent from her stay in hospital.

As she entered the bedroom she saw his jacket already casually thrown onto the bed. She could hear the thunder of water in the voluminous spa bath.

A shudder ran through her. What if he changed his mind and decided to join her in the bath? A throb pulled deep inside her womb at the thought, even as her mind insisted its denial. She forced her feet toward the bathroom. Luc was bent over the bath, pouring a splash of perfumed bath foam into the water and swirling it with a sweep of his hand. She watched as he inhaled the fragrance, the expression of sheer longing on his face striking hard to her core.

She hadn't stopped to think how this had all been for him. To be married and then to have lost her to this frozen wasteland of not remembering even the smallest thing about their life together.

"I've missed this," he said as she entered the spacious room. His voice dropped an octave. "I've missed you."

"I…I'm sorry, Luc. I'm trying to remember." Her hands fisted in frustration at her sides and her voice became more insistent. "And I did! I remembered the garden. That's when the headache became unbearable."

"Don't force it, Belinda. We don't want a re-currence of your blackout. Let it come back to you in its own time." He reached down and turned off the faucet, his movements fluid—just hinting at the muscled strength beneath his clothes. "There, your bath is ready."

Without a second glance he turned away from her, pulling his shirt free of his trousers and un-buttoning it. She couldn't tear her eyes away as he shrugged the fine cotton off his shoulders exposing the long lean line of his back. His skin still held a warm golden tan. As he unbuckled his belt and unsnapped his trousers she felt a deep longing rise within her, right up until the moment he exposed the long angry scar that laid an undeniable stripe from his hip down his right leg.

She couldn't hold back the cry that broke from her lips.

"Ugly, isn't it?" Luc half turned toward her, a flash of anger sparking in his eyes. "I'm told it will fade, and this one, too—" he gestured to the surgical scar on his abdomen "—in time. But I'll always have a limp."

"Is it still painful?" Belinda managed to ask, her gaze still riveted to the wound site. A stab of guilt lanced through her. So wrapped up in her own problems, she hadn't considered what he'd physically been through.

"Sometimes it's worse than others," he

admitted flatly before reaching into the shower to turn on the water. "Go on. Enjoy your bath."

He stepped into the large shower cubicle, and she watched as the water cascaded over his body, rivulets running through the light dusting of hair on his chest and arrowing down lower, past his taut stomach. Even though he'd obviously lost some weight in hospital, he still had a commandingly powerful build. As he lathered shower gel over his skin, she suddenly wished she'd had the courage to join him in the shower. To be the one stroking the glistening liquid soap down his chest and across the ridged hardness of his abdomen, and lower.

A flush of heat suffused her body. What was she thinking? Only hours ago she'd been terrified at the prospect of travelling with him, of leaving the virtual safety of her hospital room. Now here she was, little more than an opportunistic voyeur as he luxuriated under the pounding water of his shower.

She wheeled about and focused instead on the bath he'd drawn for her. She needed to twist her hair up, and unerringly she opened the correct drawer where her hair accessories were lined up. It should give her some comfort, she decided, that she instinctively knew where such things were. With a modicum of movement she pinned her hair up, undressed and lowered herself into the warm fragrant water. As the foaming bubbles closed over her body, she relaxed. They offered her some privacy for when Luc came out of the shower, but something inside her begged to attract his attention, something she couldn't control.

And that, right now, was her greatest fear. She didn't recognise the woman who'd fallen in love with Luc Tanner and agreed to marry him. Clearly it wasn't the Belinda Wallace she believed herself to be.

Something within her had changed in the past several months. Something drastic. It had seen her uplift herself from her home in Auckland, from her family and from her career. To give all that up for him.

She sank lower in the bath, covering her shoulders and stretching her long legs out before her. As she looked out the window over the valley, bathed in the start of a glorious sunset with swaths of red and purple creeping across the sky, she acknowledged she owed it to herself, and to Luc, to remember what that was.

Four

Despite the misgivings that plagued her about how she'd handle Luc's exit from the shower, she was surprised to find that it all felt almost impossibly familiar. Even so, tension gripped her shoulders and she pushed her head back against the built-in cushion on the side of the bath, closing her eyes the moment she'd heard him snap off the water and push open the shower door.

Her active imagination painted a very clear picture of how he looked as she heard him drag one of the thick white bath towels from the heated rail and cast it across his body to dry himself. She counted to one hundred, very slowly, before she opened her eyes again.

Luc stood at the vanity, the towel riding low on his hips, his cane resting against the blush-coloured marble countertop. She watched as he smoothed shaving cream across the hard angles of his shadowed jaw and picked up his razor. There was something incredibly sexy about watching a man shave, Belinda decided as she found herself captured by his every movement.

She must have stirred because suddenly he turned and caught her watching him. A slow smile pulled at his lips, a smile that melted her right through to her core.

"Enjoying the bath?" His eyes glowed as he took in the curve of her shoulder, the sweep of her arm as it rested along the edge of the tub and back up again to her throat where her pulse beat rapidly in the slender column of her neck.

If he'd have traced his fingertips along the

same path she couldn't have felt it more distinctly. Beneath the froth her breasts ached, her nipples tightened and her inner muscles clenched in response.

"Mmm, wonderful," she managed, but as she gazed at him she found herself referring more to the vision of male than the silky-soft environment in which she reclined.

"Hungry?" he asked, sending her mind into overdrive before she realised that she was, indeed, starving.

"Yes, I suppose I'd better get out."

"No, don't bother. I'll check first to see if dinner's ready yet." He swiped at his face with a small towel and dropped it into a laundry hamper on his way out of the bathroom.

When he returned he pushed a small wheeled trolley with one hand. As he drew closer to the bath, Belinda spied a large ceramic platter and an ice bucket containing a bottle of one of the Hawke's Bay region's finest sauvignon blancs.

Two elegantly cut crystal wineglasses stood beside the ice bucket.

"You look like you've done this before," Belinda commented as Luc extracted the bottle from the ice and deftly wiped it with a crisp white serviette.

"I've done some waiting in my time," Luc replied guardedly.

He poured two glasses of wine and handed one to her, then pulled up the vanity stool next to the bath and sat down. His towel dropped away at the side, revealing the length of his right leg—exposing the angry scar. She averted her gaze to stare out the window and past the darkening valley to where the final remnants of the sun slipped beyond the last hill. His very nearness, and nakedness, played havoc with her heart rate. Even the warmth emanating from his body tempted and tormented her.

Belinda focussed on taking a sip of the pale

straw-coloured wine, letting the perfectly chilled tropical fruit flavours roll over her tongue and down her throat. She knew from what memory she still clung to with an iron grip that no one else had ever elicited such a powerful reaction from her before.

Was this what had bound her to Luc? The overwhelming physical awareness that simmered constantly beneath the surface?

"Here, try this," Luc said, interrupting her thoughts.

Belinda turned her head toward him, to the morsel of provolone cheese encased in a sliver of prosciutto he offered. Obediently she opened her mouth. If she'd thought for even a minute that she'd regained control of her equilibrium around Luc it was shattered the instant his fingertips touched her lips. Tiny shocks buzzed across her skin at the fleeting contact as the flavours exploded in her mouth.

"Good?" he asked.

"Mmm, delicious. But, Luc, you don't need to wait on me," she protested.

"I know," he answered simply. "Indulge me." He dipped a slice of crusty bread in aioli. "Here, try this. It's Didier's own recipe and made with product sourced solely from Tautara Estate."

As he brought the morsel to her mouth a drop of oil fell and pooled in the curve of her collarbone right where it met her shoulder.

"Ah, we can't have that," Luc murmured.

He leaned forward, his tongue darting across her skin to lick up the single drop. Every muscle in her body coiled tight and she nearly shot out the water at the exquisitely brief caress. Her fingers curled tight around the stem of her wineglass, and she had to consciously stop the reflexive jerk that threatened to snap the delicate stem.

"More?" His lips were by her ear, his breath fanning the suddenly hyperresponsive skin of her neck.

"M-more?" She could barely get the single syllable past her tightened throat.

"Antipasto." Again his breath was a stroke of heated air over her skin.

"I—"

"Try this."

Helpless to do anything but open her mouth, she accepted the slice of marinated artichoke heart. Slowly he offered more bite-size delectable delights interspersed only with sips of wine.

Luc carried their conversation, keeping things general. Aside from that one time he'd licked the oil from her skin he didn't touch her again and, she was shocked to realise, she wanted him to. Oh, how she wanted him to.

When her glass was empty he took it from her and replaced it on the trolley, then leaning heavily on his cane he rose to his feet.

"Our main meal will be ready now. I'll leave you to get dried and dressed, unless you'd like some help."

Luc looked down upon her in the cooling water of the tub. A pulse throbbed at the side of his neck. A fine sheen of perspiration glistened on his brow. It gave her some relief to know that he was as similarly affected as she by the intimacy of their situation.

"No, I can manage. Thanks."

"Good. Don't be too long. I meant what I said about you not being out of my sight."

"Within reason, of course," Belinda felt compelled to add, suddenly desperate for some control of her racing pulse and the heady sense of seduction he'd transfused through her.

"Belinda, when it comes to you I'm not a reasonable man. Don't keep me waiting." His green eyes flared with heat and a self-deprecating smile pulled at his lips.

She stared at the door for several minutes after it closed behind him. His words carried more than a warning. There was an implied threat underwriting his statement, a threat that made her near uncontrollable physical reaction to him a risk to her precarious equilibrium.

He was a conundrum, sending conflicting messages that alternately confused and calmed her. The man who'd shared the antipasto with her was completely inverse to the man who'd brought her home from the hospital today, or the one who'd been at her side when she'd fainted in the herb garden. But which one was the real Luc Tanner? Which one was the man she'd fallen in love with?

By the time Belinda had dried herself and slipped through to the dressing room to select some clothes, Luc was waiting for her in the bedroom. He'd dressed casually in black jeans and a black polo shirt, and the colour made his eyes appear even greener than usual. Her breath caught in her throat at the sight of him. Starkly handsome, he was both beautiful and terrifying to behold.

She nervously smoothed her hands over the

caramel-coloured linen trousers she'd teamed with the cream silk top she'd chosen.

"Will this do?" she asked, uncomfortable under his silent scrutiny.

"You look beautiful in anything. Come. Manu has set the table for us on our deck so we can enjoy the summer evening while it lasts."

Belinda followed him through to the living room and out the open French doors. Burning tapers attached to the deck lit a table set with white linen and gleaming silverware. Heated chafing dishes sat on a smaller table to one side, alongside them a colourful tossed salad. For a moment she felt as though she'd stepped into a fairy tale.

Everything was magically perfect—the setting, the darkened valley with the peppering of lights from the far distant Taupo township on its periphery. Even the gentle strains of her favourite opera piped through the ceiling-mounted speakers in the eaves over the deck. It was almost surreal, but the aromas from the chafing dishes gave her a reality check. Not even in her dreams had she smelled anything so divine.

"I told Manu we'd serve ourselves tonight," Luc said, slipping back the cover on one of the dishes to expose tiny gourmet potatoes garnished with fresh chopped chives and handing Belinda a gold-rimmed plate.

Her experienced eye recognised the pattern of the fine imported china. Was it one they'd chosen together, or was it just a normal part of Luc's everyday life?

"You're frowning. Trying to remember again?" Luc's voice cut across her thoughts.

"I recognise this china. Did we choose it?"

Surprise flitted through his eyes, but was swiftly veiled before he spoke. "Yes, we did. You helped me outfit most of our suite before the wedding. It was important to you."

And he'd encouraged her, she was sure of it. She had a sense that he'd been prepared to do anything to keep her here—to make Tautara Estate her home as much as it was indelibly his.

"I know." She hesitated a moment, then continued. "I don't remember, but in here—" she pressed her hand against her chest "—I know."

Luc didn't speak straightaway, but Belinda couldn't help but notice the sudden tension in his shoulders or the way his eyebrows drew together. Eventually he spoke. "That's excellent. You're making great progress."

Did his hand shake ever so slightly as he dished up for them both? Chiding herself for being fanciful, she applied herself to savouring the grilled trout fillets drizzled with a subtly herbed sauce, baby potatoes and fresh salad greens with the rest of their bottle of wine. It had been so long since she'd had anything with such delicate flavour. If she never tasted a bite of hospital food again it would be too soon. They ate in comparative silence, a silence that could have been awkward but for the beauty of the velvet-dark vista spread out before them.

"It's so beautiful here." She sighed. "How do you ever tear yourself away?"

"Sometimes business requires it. For the most part I'm more than happy to remain here. Tautara Estate comprises 6,500 hectares. There's always plenty to do." He smiled as Belinda fought back a yawn. "Why don't we call it a night? You've had a tiring day, and I have to admit I could use the rest myself."

"Your leg is sore?" Belinda felt a sudden surge of guilt.

"No more than usual," Luc replied with a wave of his hand, dismissing her care.

"Is there anything I can do for you?"

Luc's lips firmed into a straight line and she sensed rather than heard his sigh.

"No. Just be yourself," he replied enigmatically.

What did he mean by that, she wondered, catching the inside of her lip between her teeth as she bit back the words that would ask him precisely that. Be herself. Right now she'd give anything to know what version of "herself" he meant.

Luc leaned heavily on his cane as he stood to get up from the table. She caught the fleeting grimace of pain he swiftly tried to mask.

Was this the way it had always been between them? Him hiding his true feelings and thoughts? She couldn't imagine that she'd have fallen in love with or married a man who was so closed to her emotionally. It just wasn't her style. Her family had always been demonstrative, affectionate. They shared their worries and concerns between them—a problem shared is halved, her father always said.

Did she and Luc have that kind of marriage? Something inside her whispered to the contrary, and the inner voice was distinctly unsettling.

Five

When they returned to their private suite, Belinda's nerves were strung out to screaming point. Inside the bedroom the drapes had been drawn, and the bedside lamps cast a warm inviting glow over the expansive bed. A bed she was now about to share with her husband. Someone had been in the room and dispensed with the throw pillows adorning the head of the bed and had turned down the sheets. A single perfect deep-pink rose stood in a bud vase on the bedside table.

The reality of sleeping with Luc bore down on her with terrifying pressure. Her heart jumped erratically in her chest and she fought to keep her breathing measured. Could she do this? Lord, she didn't even know which side of the bed he slept on. As if he read her thoughts, Luc gave her a small smile.

"You usually sleep there." He indicated the side of the bed where the vase stood. "Although I'm happy to change if it makes you feel more comfortable."

Twin beds would make her feel more comfortable right now, Belinda decided. Even separate rooms. She drew in a levelling breath and forced herself to meet his gaze.

"No, that will be fine. If that's the way we've always done it."

Luc's smile froze on his face for the briefest moment before he nodded.

"Belinda—" The chime of his cell phone interrupted what he'd been about to say. He flicked a glance at the caller ID. "Excuse me. I need to take this. I might be a while."

Belinda watched as he left the room, his murmured tones disappearing behind the closed door. She hurried to the dressing room and grabbed a ruby-coloured nightgown from one of her drawers. With more haste than care she shucked off her clothing and pulled it on. The gown was a filmy piece of next to nothing, with a soft stretch lace bodice that hugged her breasts like a lover's caress.

She smoothed her hand down over the gossamer-fine material and wondered if she had bought the nightgown as part of her trousseau or whether it had been a gift from Luc. The very idea of his hands caressing the fabric the way her own did now sent a perverse thrill of longing through her body.

What was wrong with her? Inside her mind she reacted like a frightened virgin, yet physically her body yearned for Luc's touch. Belinda shook her head and hurried to the bathroom. Every step of today had brought her nothing but more questions. She was weary of it all. Bone weary. Suddenly that big, softly lit bed was very inviting indeed.

Catching her reflection in the bathroom mirror, Belinda wondered whether she shouldn't have simply chosen a T-shirt to sleep in instead. The tiny spaghetti straps looped over her shoulders lent an impression of wanton fragility, and the warmth of the red fabric made her skin glow like that of a woman welcoming her lover. Belinda huffed in frustration. She was driving herself crazy and it had to stop.

She seated herself at the vanity and grabbed a hairbrush from the drawer and started to brush her long dark hair with punishing strokes.

A movement in the doorway stilled her hand. Luc stepped forward and took her hairbrush from her fingers. "Are you trying to rip it all out?" His censure was as gentle as his touch as he took over from where she'd begun.

"I thought you might have been in bed already," he commented, his eyes meeting hers in the mirror.

So he'd recognised her sudden fear. He knew her better than she gave him credit for, but then, of course he would. Right now he knew her better than she knew herself. Sudden tears of frustration sprang to her eyes.

Luc stopped brushing, his hands settling on her shoulders.

"Belinda?"

She blinked away the burning moisture, breaking eye contact with him. He saw far too much.

"I'm okay. Just tired, that's all."

"Understandable. It's been a full day, for both of us." He took her hand and helped her to her feet. "Go to bed. I'll be along in a while."

She couldn't decide whether she was

relieved or disappointed that he wasn't coming to bed now.

"Aren't you tired, too?" she asked.

"Yes, but something's come up. Guests we weren't expecting until late next week have brought their trip forward to the day after tomorrow. Manu and I have some contingency plans to lay in place."

"Guests? Already?"

"It's not ideal, but they can't be put off. They should only be here a couple of nights."

"They're regulars?"

"After a fashion, yes."

"Then they'll have certain expectations. We must meet them. You can't give them less than that. You wouldn't under normal circumstances," she said carefully.

Right now Belinda couldn't think of anything worse, but this was Luc's business. The fact he'd cancelled out six weeks of patronage for their honeymoon—six weeks they'd lost—meant he would have to get back to business. Besides, the sooner she resumed life as she'd known it, the sooner she might start to remember.

"Spoken like a true hotelier's daughter. We'll worry about it in the morning. Now, go to bed."

He dropped a fleeting kiss on her forehead and turned her toward the bedroom, following close on her heels. When she was settled in the bed, he switched off the lamp nearest her. Belinda suddenly reached out and held his arm.

"Please, leave the other light on until you come to bed?"

"It won't disturb you?"

"No. I grew used to a light in the hospital." She stifled a yawn. "Besides, I doubt anything could keep me awake now."

Challenging heat flared in Luc's eyes and Belinda felt an answering response in her body. The elasticized bodice of her nightwear felt too small as her nipples hardened and pressed against the fabric.

Well, maybe there was one thing. As wrong as this all felt to her she couldn't deny there was a powerful magnetic pull between them. Luc straightened and trailed his hand over her shoulder and down her arm, leaving her skin tingling beneath his fleeting touch.

She barely heard the click of the door as it closed behind him. A near overwhelming desire to call him back choked in her throat as Belinda silently admitted she'd never felt so completely lost and alone in her entire life.

The meeting with Manu had been productive, and Luc let himself back into their suite with a tired sigh of relief. Their guests would arrive the day after tomorrow around lunchtime, in time for drinks followed by an al fresco luncheon on the deck. Then, if Belinda was up to it, she'd accompany the female member of the party to Taupo by helicopter for a couple of hours' shopping while he and Manu took her husband fly-fishing in one of the rivers that ran through the property.

The female member.

Luc clenched his jaw against the curse that fought to rip from his throat. He had no doubt that Demi Le Clerc had trouble up her sleeve when she'd had her assistant phone the estate to change her booking. His unease had magnified when Manu reported he'd tried to contact the award-winning jazz singer to inform her that the booking couldn't be altered but apparently she and her new fiancé were "in transit" and therefore unavailable. With modern communication being what it was, Luc very much doubted she was unreachable, rather that she'd informed her staff of her intention to be that way. How she'd found out so quickly that he'd returned home said a great deal for her spy network.

Manu had already agreed to check amongst the staff to find out if that particular spy network had been fed by one of their own. Confidentiality and loyalty were sacrosanct. If anyone had abused either, they were in breach of their employment contract and would be dispensed with immediately.

Luc swallowed against the bitter taste in his mouth when he thought of Demi and Belinda meeting. He was reluctant to expose her to Belinda while his wife was still in such a vulnerable position, but then, it may well work to his advantage. What harm could Demi possibly do when Belinda remembered nothing of their time together? Belinda had no idea their marriage had been the catalyst that had seen Demi break tabloid records with the speed of her engagement to aging billionaire oilman Hank Walker.

He'd been a fool to ever let Demi think there was more to their relationship than casual friendship. He'd never once entertained the idea of marrying her, despite her attempts to entice him into commitment. They'd made love just the once—a coupling that provided physical release only, with little else to recommend it.

Luc moved restlessly toward his piano in the dimly lit room. He was too wound up to sleep. He closed his eyes and let his fingers drift gently across the keys, the haunting quality of the music he played flowed over him—relaxing his muscles and his mind.

Playing had always had that effect on him, even back in his teens, although he was never the kind of teenager who'd have admitted to this particular skill. No, hotwiring cars and breaking and entering were more his style then. It had been during a B&E that he'd been sprung by the owner of the house—an elderly gentleman who'd seen right through Luc's attitude and invited him back, through the front door next time. It had taken six weeks but Luc had found his feet retracing the path to Mr. Hensen's home. The retired pianist had sensed Luc needed an outlet, a change of direction in his path of self-destruction. He'd insisted on giving Luc lessons—lessons that had been emphatically refused until the threat of going to the police was coolly raised.

It had been ages since Luc had thought about Mr. Hensen. Ages since he'd allowed himself to miss the old man in a way he'd never missed his parents after their deaths.

As the final note hung on the air, Luc let his eyes open again. Belinda sat opposite him on one of the large cream sofas, her feet curled under her. His eyes raked over her barely clad body, his pulse leaping to instant life. It had been torture to leave her in bed, her body gilded by the bedside lamp, her hair a glorious fan across the fine linen of her pillowcase. He'd wanted to make love with her with a physical ache that had almost driven him to his knees—to imprint himself back in her mind and her body in a way she would never forget again.

He dragged his wayward thoughts under disciplined restraint. Luc Tanner hadn't gotten where he was today by giving in to impulse. No, everything about his life was about control. He'd learned the hard way what a lack of power did to a person, how it demeaned them—rendered them helpless victims. The helpless had no respect in this world. Pity, yes. But he'd had his fill of pity and well-meaning intentions. Now he commanded respect in all walks of his life.

"You play beautifully," Belinda said, her voice hesitant, as if she sensed the power play going on inside him.

"I didn't mean to wake you."

"You didn't. I guess I'm too used to the disruptions and noise of the hospital. The quiet, of all things, woke me. A bit later I heard you on the piano. Did your meeting with Manu go well?"

"Yes, everything's organised. Are you sure you're okay with this? I can have them rerouted to another property if necessary."

"Luc, when I couldn't get back to sleep I started to think about a few things, and to be honest, as terrifying as it is, I have to get back into my old life if I'm going to move forward. I can't turn back time and see what happened before, but I can't stay stagnant like this, either. It's driving me crazy. Everything around me—" she waved her arm to encapsulate the room "—it's all new, yet sometimes familiar at the same time. Even the music you played. I know you've played it for me before, haven't you?"

"I have."

Luc swallowed. Yes, he'd played it for her before. The last time had been the night he'd proposed. They'd spent a day out on the estate together, made love together for the first time on the riverbank during a picnic—his body tightened in remembrance of her welcoming embrace, at how she'd uninhibitedly given herself fully to him. He'd instantly become addicted to her in a way he'd never imagined possible.

He'd never wanted anyone or anything in his life as much as he wanted her. The truth had frightened him until he'd persuaded himself it was because she was the perfect accompaniment to the world he'd built. He couldn't have been thinking of anything else. By the time they'd driven back to the house, he'd decided to step up his plans and propose to her earlier than he'd anticipated. He still remembered the surge of triumph when she'd said yes.

They'd fallen to the floor, right here in this sitting room, and made love again to seal their betrothal. All she'd worn for the next twenty-four hours had been the blue diamond engagement ring he'd had made for her months earlier.

"Will you play something else for me now?" Belinda's voice dragged him back from the past.

"Another time," he said, rising from the piano bench and grabbing his cane.

He offered her his hand to pull her to her feet, and they went through to the bedroom together.

By the time he'd undressed and was ready for bed she was curled on her side of the bed, her eyes closed, her breathing even.

She'd fallen asleep after all. But as he slid between the cool cotton of the sheets, she rolled over to face him, her blue-grey eyes massive in her heart-shaped face.

"Luc?"

He lifted a hand to smooth away a strand of her hair that fell across her cheek. "Hmmm?"

"What I said before…" She closed her eyes and took in a deep breath. "What I said before about getting back into my old life—I meant *every* aspect of my old life. Obviously we're not strangers to each other. Whenever I look at you my body tells me that."

So she still felt the same inexorable pull between them. Luc suppressed the smile of satisfaction that threatened to spread across his face at her words.

He watched as she moistened her lips with

the tip of her tongue, clearly choosing her next words carefully.

"Well, what I mean is…if you want to… y'know. Maybe it'll help." Her words faded away into the expanding silence of the room.

Luc traced the curve of her brow, then the sweep of her cheekbone with one finger, before bringing it to rest at the cupid's bow of her lips. He'd wanted her to come to him willingly and now she had. Something foreign warmed and bloomed deep inside him.

"No," he said quietly, his negative response surprising even himself.

"You don't want me?" She sounded hurt and relieved at the same time.

"Oh, I want you. When the time is right we will make love again. But tonight isn't that time. When we make love it won't be because you want to remember, but because you do."

Was that relief in her eyes or disappointment? He leaned forward and took her lips gently with his own, holding back the beast that clawed within him to plunder their generous softness. As much as it tormented him, he would wait.

She sighed softly against his lips. "Good night, Luc."

She rolled over to her other side, and Luc curved his arm around her, pulling her in close against the hardness of his body. He felt her stiffen as the evidence of his arousal nestled along the crease of her buttocks, then felt her relax into him as the truth of his obvious desire for her sank in, secure in the knowledge his rejection of her wasn't because he didn't want her.

He lay there for hours, his eyes burning in the dark as she slid into a deep sleep. Her body shaped to his. His instincts screamed to take her and brand her his once more. It would be the ultimate satisfaction, when she remembered everything, for her to know she hadn't been able to resist him. But he'd meant what he'd said before. When she made love with him again it would be because she remembered what their lovemaking had been like, how it had become a compulsion neither of them could deny. How they'd both resented everything that had come between their opportunities to be alone together. If he could do anything in his power to encourage that memory, he would.

The intense satisfying physicality of their relationship had been an unexpected bonus. An indicator, of sorts, that he'd been right all along when he'd decided to make Belinda Wallace his wife and mistress of Tautara Lodge.

His life—his plan—would carry on as before. The hiccup of their accident would fade into a minor blip on the radar of his success.

Six

The next morning Belinda awoke feeling more rested than she had in ages. But with the fresh light of the morning, and the cool empty sheets beside her, anxiety had reasserted itself once more.

Where had the trepidation she'd felt when she'd first seen him at the hospital gone? She'd been forced into close contact with him yesterday—a close contact she hadn't questioned and which, to be totally honest, had felt right. Was this how victims of Stockholm Syndrome felt? Had that been Luc's intention all along—to make her completely reliant on him so far away from what little familiarity she had?

Aside from the obvious, the fact she couldn't remember what was a very important part of her life, why did she still feel as though there was something more overshadowing her mind's refusal to recall her memories. Even now, as she approached Luc at the dining table, where he sat reading a paper over breakfast, she sensed a closed door deep inside of him, a part of him that lay deep in shadow, and she wanted to know what was behind that door.

The only way she would find out was to keep going. He was her husband. She owed it to them both. Belinda painted a smile on her face and forced herself not to smooth the short-sleeved top she'd pulled on over designer jeans one more time as Luc looked up.

"Good morning," Luc said, folding his paper neatly and putting it to one side. "You slept well?"

"Very well." A faint rush of heat bloomed

across her cheeks as she recalled how his enveloping arms had held her against him, how her body had reacted to his touch.

"Good." Luc gave a nod of satisfaction. "Since we're technically working from tomorrow, I've planned some fun for us today."

"Fun? That sounds intriguing. What have you got in mind?"

Belinda reached for the coffee carafe and poured Luc another cup. She was halfway through pouring when her hand suddenly shook.

"I'm sorry, I didn't ask if you wanted another." She stopped pouring and rested the carafe on a place mat on the table.

Luc gave her a searching look. "I always have two cups at breakfast."

The ramifications of Luc's reply echoed through her mind. She instinctively remembered that, but she didn't remember him? How labyrinthine could the mind get? Her neurologist had spoken to her at length about the voids in her memory and how simple everyday matters could appear, as this one had this morning. Being here—being with Luc—obviously stimulated the part of her mind that held her memory captive.

Luc placed his hand over hers, where it rested on the handle of the carafe. She fought not to flinch from his touch, from the spark of physical recognition that relentlessly spiralled through her every time he was near.

"You remembered that without trying. Don't over analyse it. Just let it come."

"How can I do that when I don't know the difference between remembering and not?" Her voice shook slightly.

"We'll find a balance. Don't worry. Who knows what might happen today."

He let go of her hand, took a swig of his coffee, then rose from the table.

"Where are we going?"

"I thought we'd take a trip around parts of

the estate today. Play hooky." He gave her a smile. "Are you up for it?"

A sensation, not unlike fear, snaked along her spine. She couldn't help but feel he had a hidden agenda to his suggestion.

"Just the two of us?" she asked.

"Does that bother you?"

"No, it doesn't bother me. Should it?" She forced her lips into a smile.

Luc's eyes narrowed as her question hung on the air. "If you'd rather stay here at the lodge today, that's okay."

"No, no! Going out today would be fabulous."

"Well, if it assuages your fears any, Manu will be driving us." He rose to his feet and snatched his cane up from by the table.

"I could drive," Belinda offered.

Luc halted midstride. His face paled measurably and he gave her a searching look that made her heart stutter in her chest. What had she said wrong?

"Or not." She attempted to lighten the air that had suddenly frozen between them with glacial coolness.

"I think not. Not yet, anyway." Luc appeared to have recovered his equilibrium and his skin recovered its usual hue. "How soon can you be ready?"

Belinda flicked a glance at the clock above the kitchen stove. "Give me ten minutes, then I'm all yours."

"*All* mine?" Luc's voice deepened and Belinda was suddenly swept with an uneasy sense of déjà vu.

She put out a hand and grasped a chair back to steady herself. Tiny black dots danced before her eyes. She forced herself to breathe, drawing air into her lungs and expelling it again with careful deliberation. She felt Luc's hand at her back—a reassurance that lent her much-needed strength.

"You okay?" His breath stirred the hair at her nape.

"Yeah," she said on shaky breath. "I'll be fine. I'll go and get ready."

"Make sure you grab a jacket in case it gets cool later, and wear comfortable walking shoes, okay?"

"We'll be out all day?"

"If you're up for it."

She let go of the chair and stepped out of his reach. "I'm up for it."

"I'll meet you out front."

By the time she'd splashed her face and reapplied her makeup, she was heading closer to fifteen minutes than the ten she'd promised, but as she joined Luc at the front door she had at least regained most of her equilibrium. It niggled at her that he hadn't been keen for her to drive. She'd held her licence since her late teens and had always been a good driver, but he'd looked sick to his stomach at the prospect.

Ah, well, she sighed, at least this way she'd get to enjoy the countryside a bit more than if she had to concentrate on the roads.

She was surprised when Luc sat in the back beside her as they headed off, and said as much. Luc responded by linking his fingers through hers and answering, "I've been forced to be apart from you for too long already. Why wouldn't I want to be by my wife's side?"

There was an intensity to his words that both soothed and unnerved her. She gave herself an internal shake. What was wrong with her? Everything she felt at the moment was a contradiction to what she'd felt only a moment ago. And underlying it all was the insidious awareness that something wasn't right, that somehow she was living the wrong life. Maybe she should have let Luc call the doctor yesterday. This weird sense of displacement, the inherent sense of wrongness couldn't be normal.

Luc dragged her attention to the land that spread out before them and described the extent of the estate's farming and forestry operations, as they followed the road down the side of the hill, going deeper into the valley with every kilometre. As far as she could see in any direction the land was entailed in Tautara Estate. She started to get a new appreciation of how vast her husband's business interest here was and how many staff he employed.

"And Luc is being modest," Manu interrupted as he negotiated a hairpin bend in the road. "We offer some of the best fishing and hunting grounds in the whole of New Zealand, and for the adventurous they can go rafting, too."

"Sounds like you offer it all," Belinda commented.

"Yeah, well, we aim to please, don't we, mate?" Manu's gaze flicked to the rearview mirror, his eyes crinkled with the smile that wreathed his face.

"We do at that," Luc answered enigmatically, and gave Belinda's hand a gentle squeeze.

After just over an hour they reached a clearing and Manu pulled the four-wheel-drive vehicle in and parked, leaping down to open Belinda's door for her before she could alight.

"Here you are. I'll head on as we discussed this morning, okay?"

"Thanks, Manu," Luc answered.

"Are you sure you'll be okay?" There was a note of concern in the other man's voice that alerted Belinda he was not entirely happy to be leaving them here.

"I'll be fine. Don't worry. Besides, I've got this and I've got the two-way." Luc lifted his cane slightly with one hand and patted the small radio clipped to his belt with the other. "I'll call you if I need you."

"Make sure he does." Manu turned to Belinda, the serious light in his eyes telling her unreservedly that he wasn't kidding. "I mean it, if he looks like he's in any pain at all, call me."

"Stop fussing, Manu." Irritation laced Luc's words with acerbity.

"You call being sensible, fussing? Her with

her blackout yesterday, you with your hip, both of you just out of hospital and now me leaving you both in the wilderness. I need my head read is what."

Though he tried to inject some humour into his voice Belinda could see he was genuinely worried. She put her hand out to him, gripping his forearm and meeting his worried gaze full-on.

"I will look after him, don't worry. And if I feel like I can't manage, either him or myself, Luc will call you. Okay?"

"S'pose it'll have to be. Right, then, catch you later."

Still muttering, Manu climbed back into the four-by-four and wheeled back out onto the private road, heading off in the same direction they'd been travelling.

"He has a point." Belinda turned to Luc. "We pretty much are the walking wounded."

"Are you worried?" He gave her a searching look.

"No, not at all. In fact it's great to be out in the fresh air. Away from walls."

"I know what you mean. If you want to head back at any stage just tell me."

"I'll be fine," she said with emphasis on the "I," and left unsaid the query as to whether he could manage. It was clear his strength was an issue of pride; she didn't want to aggravate him with her concern any more than Manu already had.

"We'll both be fine. The walk is level and there are plenty of rest stops on the way. C'mon."

Luc took her by the hand and led her along a well- trodden trail that wound alongside a bubbling river. All around them the sounds of bird life and the ever-present hum of cicadas filled the air. The air was warm and a soft breeze played in the trees. She was glad they'd left their jackets in the car. Despite her earlier fears, Belinda felt herself begin to relax. They took their time, and Luc paused every fifteen minutes or so to point out items of interest—a particular indigenous plant he knew she'd delight in, or the movement of fish in the water.

At one point Luc pulled her down to sit with him on a large fallen tree.

"Let's rest awhile," Luc said, rubbing absently at his hip as he propped his cane beside him.

"Is your leg bothering you?" Belinda wondered just how much pain he was in.

"A little," he admitted. "I'll be fine after a bit of a rest."

"Are you sure?"

"Of course I'm sure. Besides, it never hurts to stop and just enjoy the scenery from time to time."

Belinda's cheeks flushed under the heat in his gaze. Judging by his intensely focused look, he wasn't talking about the riverbank or its surroundings. Luc lifted a hand to smooth her hair away from her face, and his fingers slid along her scalp to cup the back of her head.

"Tell me you don't want me to do this."

His face drew closer, his lips parted ever so

slightly. The air around them thickened. Sound retreated. The distance between them closed. Even if she'd been capable of denying him she very much doubted she would.

Without conscious thought she closed the distance between them. His lips were firm and dry as they captured hers, and her senses leaped to sudden and demanding life. When Luc's fingers tightened on the back of her head, she sank into him, her arms snaking around his waist, her breasts pressing against the hard wall of his chest.

Whatever uncertainties plagued her she couldn't deny the absolute synchronicity of their physical sense of belonging. Belinda gave herself over to sensation as Luc deepened their kiss. A flame of want kindled deep inside her, pressing her closer against him, welcoming his touch and taste with a sense of homecoming that was as fundamental in its origin as the rising sun each morning.

When Luc pulled away, his breathing was

rapid and his eyes shone with the burning clarity of desire. She should feel intimidated by that look, Belinda told herself. She should be telling him "no more." Instead, her body clamored for his touch, her lips ached for more of the fierce pressure of his lips. She was surprised when he pushed up to his feet and stood, with his hands planted on his hips, and looked out over the river, away from her.

When he turned he was back under control. The light in his eyes had dulled, his breathing returned to normal.

"Shall we go on?"

Confused, Belinda stood and brushed the remnants of bark from the seat of her jeans before answering. "Sure. Let's go." What had made him pull back like that? She could have sworn he was as lost in their kiss as she'd been.

Again Luc took her hand, and as they continued on the path, she noticed he leaned more heavily on the cane than he had before.

"Is it much further?" she asked.

"Just around the next bend in the river," Luc replied, his words clipped.

Belinda stopped in her tracks. "What is it? Why are you angry?" She was talking to his back as he doggedly kept walking.

"It's nothing. Let's carry on."

"Is it your leg? Because I don't mind resting a bit longer before we carry on. It's been a long time since I've exerted myself this much, and I could do with the rest."

He stopped and turned to face her, his expression raw with something she couldn't quite define.

"No, it's not my leg."

"Then what is it? Was it the kiss? Did you want me to say no?"

"It wasn't that. It's nothing you can do anything about in your current state. Just leave it." He turned back and started walking again.

Belinda huffed in exasperation. He'd closed

up as effectively as a bank vault under siege. There was nothing else for it but to follow him, but instead she stayed right where she was, chewing over his words as she did so. "In her current state." What the heck had he meant by that? Obviously her amnesia was as frustrating to him as to her, but he had the advantage of remembering their life together—of remembering their love.

For her the only thing she knew was that she desired him, and that was terrifying enough. She'd never been the type to embark on a frivolous relationship, and took the physical side of a relationship very seriously.

If she listened to her body, they would already be lovers again—even though he was a stranger to her. It went against everything she believed in, but she couldn't deny the truth—not when her blood raced hot and demanding through her body and her core ached with an emptiness she knew only he could fill.

Her cheeks coloured as she remembered again his rejection of her last night. She kicked a stone off the path and watched it tumble down the bank and into the river and sighed helplessly.

"I'm sorry."

Luc's voice from close behind her made her jump and turn. He placed his forefinger on her lips, preventing her from speaking.

"Yes, I am sore. Yes, it was that kiss. And yes, I want you more than I've ever wanted you before. But I know what our marriage meant to you. I want that back. I want it all back before I make love with you again. That's why I'm in a foul mood."

Belinda's anger melted in the face of his honesty. It was clear how much it had cost him to bare his emotions like that. Sharp lines bracketed his mouth, his eyebrows were drawn in a harsh straight line, his fist clenched on the top of his cane.

"I'm sorry, too. I forget that I'm not the only one who's lost something here," she said, her voice shaking slightly.

She slipped an arm around his waist and together they strolled in silence along the path. As they came into another clearing Belinda gasped in surprise. Ahead of them a green-and-white-striped canvas canopy had been erected over a wooden table and two matching chairs. An ice bucket, with a bottle of champagne cooling within it, sat in the centre and was surrounded by a series of covered dishes. A long-stemmed rosebud, this time an intense coral colour, stood in a bud vase next to the ice bucket. Beside the table a sumptuous collection of pillows and fine cotton throws adorned the grass.

"You planned this all along?"

"You like it?"

"I love it. It seems so…decadent."

"It's what we specialise in. Decadence. Privacy."

* * *

Luc watched Belinda carefully. Walking away from her earlier, knowing exactly what awaited them around the corner, had been one of the hardest things he'd had to do since he'd collected her from the hospital yesterday. While he'd recuperated in hospital, he'd thought waiting patiently for her memories to return would be easy, but he was not in the mood to be patient anymore. With luck, this planned seduction, the mirror of their first time together, would be the trigger that would restore his life to the way it should have been all along. Perhaps, he dared hope, even better than before.

Seven

Belinda turned to face him. A smile of pure joy slowly wreathed her beautiful face and put a light in her blue eyes. He'd pleased her, and that pleased him. The realisation was a cold, sharp shock that sat at odds with his agenda. As did the sudden pull in the region of his chest—an expansion of warmth he'd instinctively learned to suppress as a child. A feeling he'd trained himself never to acknowledge.

"This is spectacular. Thank you." She reached up and kissed him on the cheek.

It was a peck, nothing more, yet with its innocence it stoked the fire that constantly simmered inside him. He watched as she sank down onto the bed of pillows, her hair spreading about her like a silken web of enticement.

Her T-shirt lifted slightly above her waist to expose a band of smooth creamy skin. His fingers itched to trace the inviting line. Down low his blood pooled, his body throbbed with a primal beat that threatened to dominate his careful strategy. He had to remember what had brought them together, and what had torn them apart. He had to preserve the former whatever it took.

He poured a glass of champagne, then lifted the rosebud from its vase before carefully lowering himself by her side.

"Some wine?"

He held the flute to her lips as she propped herself up a little, then took a sip of the bubbling liquid himself.

"Mmm, you said we specialise in decadence,

I can't think of anything more decadent than this right now." She sighed.

Luc raised an eyebrow and pinned her with his stare. "Really? Nothing else more decadent?"

Her laughter was unexpected, a rich cascade of joy that penetrated deep inside. And there it was again, that glimmer of warmth from within his chest, a sense of rightness. His throat dried and words failed him as he looked down at her. He couldn't help but remember the last time they'd been here. Couldn't help but want to draw that memory from deep within its prison in her mind.

He casually trailed the rosebud back and forth across the exposed skin of her belly and watched her skin twitch and contract beneath the intensely coloured petals. The contrast between the pearl-like incandescence of her skin and the vibrance of the rosebud was wickedly appealing. What would it take, he wondered, to provoke her mind? To provoke the memories of physical pleasure the touch of the rose should invoke. After their first time here she'd barely been able to look at a rosebud without a flush of desire staining her cheeks, her throat, her chest.

Under the light touch of a flower such as this, she'd revealed a sensual side of her he'd only dreamed about. It was something he'd been prepared to forgo when he'd planned to make her his wife, knowing that in every other aspect she'd be the perfect complement to his perfectly created personal sphere. Sex, to him, had always been enjoyable but never the driving force of his world—until he'd made love with Belinda for the first time, right here in this clearing.

He would coerce her into remembering. One exquisite tingling sensation at a time.

He knew it was a risk, a huge risk, but the doctors had said several times that while her memory could return at any time, it was unlikely she would remember the details of what happened immediately prior to the accident that had led to her brain injury.

Luc had built his life on risk. Today was no different.

He offered her another sip of champagne.

"To new beginnings," he toasted.

"To new beginnings," Belinda repeated and put her lips to the tilted glass, putting her hand over his as she did so.

As she tipped the glass back up and swallowed, Luc softly trailed the rosebud down over the muscles in her throat, dipping into the hollow at its base before tracing a line along her collarbone. A flush of colour stained her cheeks, and her breathing became a little uneven. She relinquished her hold over his hand and let her hand drop to her side. A shudder ran through her as he let the rose drift down to the vee of her T-shirt, to the shadowed valley of her breasts.

She drew in a sudden sharp breath, her eyes

flying to his, a stricken expression in them that made him stop what he was doing immediately and toss the rose to the blanket.

"Luc?" Her voice was unsteady.

"What is it? Are you feeling unwell?"

He dropped the flute on the grass, unheeding of the liquid as it drained into the ground, and wrapped his fingers around her hand as she reached for him. He was shocked to discover her skin was cold and clammy.

"Not unwell, exactly, just strange. Like we've done this before. It's sort of like how I felt yesterday, when I remembered about the garden, but different."

"Tell me, what do you remember?"

"I'm not sure exactly. I…I think we'd been swimming, yes, the water was freezing and you teased me about the goose bumps on my skin. Told me I was soft."

"Go on," he coaxed. Would she remember the rest? How he'd helped her from the water hole at the edge of the glade where they were now. How he'd wrapped her in a thick fluffy towel and dried her body, chafing her skin until her circulation had returned—until the light in her eyes had changed and he'd let the towel drop to the grass at their feet and lifted her into his arms and carried her to the bed of blankets and pillows just like the one they now lay on. How he'd traced every delectable line of her body with a rosebud, a yellow one that time, teasing her to a peak of aching trembling need before bringing her to the pinnacle of satisfaction with its soft-petalled touch.

Belinda remained silent. Her gazed locked on a faraway place. He watched the expressions flit across her face, the struggle as she fought to draw together the elusive threads that hovered on the periphery of her mind, then the change in her eyes, the blush of heat across her cheeks, down her throat.

She'd remembered. He'd wager the deed to

Tautara Estate that she remembered that day and what had happened next.

A fine tremor ran through her body and she turned her gaze upon him.

"It's coming back to me, Luc. I remember that day."

Luc felt the warmth begin to return to her fingers, felt them shift beneath his touch. She pulled his hand toward her and drew it to her chest.

"Can you feel my heartbeat? It's racing a million miles a minute. Luc, can you believe it? My memory is coming back."

His hand flexed beneath hers, against the softness of the fine cotton of her T-shirt, against the curve of her breast. Through the lace of her bra he felt her response to the memories, to his touch.

"Was that why you planned today like this?" she asked, leaning into the strength of his hand, allowing his palm to shape around the fullness of her breast, to feel the hardness of her nipple as it firmed and crested.

"I had to do whatever I could to get you back. I know I've been telling you not to force it, but—"

"Shh." Belinda pressed her fingers against his lips. "Don't say any more. It's okay. I know what I'm remembering now isn't everything, there are still huge gaps there. But of all the memories I've lost, this one is probably the most precious. I even remember how I felt that day, how excited I was that you'd taken the whole day off work to spend with me. How much fun we had in the water until I got too cold to stay in there any longer. Then you dried me off…"

Luc nodded slowly. Would she remember what had happened next? He wasn't disappointed.

"You…you picked me up and brought me here, laid me down on the blankets and—" She gestured to the rose on the blankets. "You made love to me, first with the rose and then you covered me with your body."

Luc shifted across the distance between them,

lowering her onto her back and sliding over her until her hips cradled his.

"Like this?"

"Yes." She sighed. "Just like that."

Beneath him she flexed her hips, pushing her mound against his now-straining erection, forcing him to swallow a groan of need.

Belinda let her eyes slide closed and shook as memories cascaded through her mind, memories and sensations that wound her body tight with need, playing like an erotic dance against the background of her consciousness. She lifted her hands to cup Luc's face between them, to draw his mouth to hers, to take his lips and delve beyond them with her questing tongue. Another shudder shook her as his tongue grazed against hers, and she relished the taste and texture of him. Relished and, she realised with a thrill of sheer pleasure, *remembered* the way he made her feel. She drove her hands up into his hair, holding him to her—terrified that if she let go, or if he broke contact, the exquisitely precious memories that flooded her mind would become as ephemeral as the gentle breeze that caressed their bodies.

Sunlight dappled against her closed lids, sending a kaleidoscope of sensuous rich reds to imprint on her retinas. Luc shifted slightly, and she moaned with pleasure as his lips trailed along her jaw, to her earlobe where he took the unadorned piece of flesh between his teeth, letting them graze softly over the surface. Then his tongue dipped into the hollow behind her ear, and her nerves jumped with pleasure.

For everything she'd forgotten it was clear he remembered it all. Remembered every tiny part of her that could send pleasure cascading through her body.

"Luc." His name was a sigh across her lips as his hands pushed up under her T-shirt, skimming the surface of her skin with a gentleness she wanted to drive to the next level. She didn't want gentle from him, not now. Not when her memory burned with the remembrance of the first time they'd made love here in this enchanted glade. Where he'd driven her body to heights she'd never dreamed possible, leaving her spent and weak in his arms before doing it all over again.

She shifted slightly as he clenched the fabric of her top in fisted hands, dragging the material up her torso and over her head, dropping it somewhere. She was beyond caring as the soft breeze stroked her skin.

"Open your eyes," his voice commanded, thick with the desire she felt surging through him like the inexorable journey of the river beside them.

She forced her heavy lids open, met his green-eyed gaze and felt the instant buzz of connection she now knew had been missing in the past twenty-four hours.

"You're mine. All mine." The words ground past his lips and she nodded.

"All yours," she whispered as he bent his head to her breasts, his teeth pulling aside the lacy cup of her bra and exposing her aching nipple to the caress of his tongue, the rasp of his teeth. A spear of pleasure shot straight to her core, and she clenched her inner muscles reflexively against the sensation, the movement setting up a ripple of smaller bursts of pleasure to thrill through her body.

Now she understood why those words had given her that shocking sense of déjà vu this morning. Why it had left her feeling as if she was a boat adrift from its moorings. He'd uttered the same words to her only months ago as he'd worshipped her body on these very blankets. But she no longer felt as if she was adrift. No, she was where she belonged, with the man to whom she belonged. Their reunion felt right on every level, and while she wanted him to hasten, to race her to the completion she knew lay on the periphery of his touch, she also wanted to savour every exquisite second.

She traced the shape of his head with her hands, stroked the cords of his neck, gripped the hard-muscled strength of his shoulders.

She was his. He was hers. How could she have forgotten such a simple truth?

Luc moved lower, his hands now splayed across her rib cage, his tongue tracing tiny circles around her belly button. She ached to feel him inside her again, to feel him fill her, complete her the way she now gloriously remembered. When his hands skimmed down to the waistband of her jeans she sighed in relief. He unsnapped her fly and pushed the denim away from her hips and down her legs.

He dipped his head lower again, his tongue dancing a tantalising line across the waistband of her panties, his hands now sliding beneath her buttocks, kneading the globes of flesh as he tilted her hips up. The contrast between the firmness of his hands and the enticing featherlight touch of his tongue as he tormented her with tiny touches sent her wild. At the tiny hollow at the top of her thighs, in the curve of her hips—everywhere but where she craved him most.

Then, gloriously, his mouth was suddenly, hotly against her. The warmth of his breath through her panties made her arch her back as sensation roared through her. She pressed against his mouth, her head thrashing from side to side, words tumbling from her lips begging him for more. His hand twisted in her underwear, tearing the fabric away from her body, baring her to his touch.

The contrast in sensation between the breeze that swept around them and the heat of his mouth as he closed over her sent a piercing shaft of desire through her. As his tongue swirled over her, at first softly then with increasing pressure, she clutched at the blankets beneath her. Her thighs trembled, and her inner muscles clenched in rhythm with his onslaught until, with a scream that tore from her throat, she went hurtling over the edge.

Luc shifted and Belinda, too boneless to do anything but watch, lay before him—her legs splayed, her skin flushed with orgasm—as he pulled off his shirt and shucked off his jeans and briefs. There was a light in his eyes that hadn't been there before. Framed by his short dark lashes, they gleamed with the heat of his need for her. A need that spiralled again within her, within seconds, as if she hadn't just climaxed moments before. As he positioned himself between her thighs again, a tremor of anticipation shivered along her spine.

"My wife." His voice was low pitched, almost guttural.

She could feel the heat of him, his blunt tip teasing her as he hesitated at her entrance.

"Luc, please," she begged, "please!"

He plunged inside her, driving himself to the hilt, and she hooked her legs around his waist, tilting her hips higher to take him in more deeply. She clung to his shoulders, near mindless with bliss as he slowly withdrew then entered her again, repeating the motion with increasing urgency until she felt him tense and shake, every muscle straining, holding back his climax. He slid one hand between them, where they were joined, before sliding his thumb across her hooded bundle of nerve endings. At his touch she felt the ripple begin within her again, this time with an even more urgent edge than before, and she clenched against him, her hips rising to meet his, forcing him to increase the pressure against her until she fractured apart. As the waves of pleasure undulated through her body, she felt his muscles bunch beneath her hands, heard his raw groan of completion as he shuddered against her over and over as the paroxysms of his pleasure rocked his body.

When he collapsed against her, Belinda could

barely breathe, but she welcomed his weight, his total possession. This was how it had been between them—she knew it at a level that was soul deep. She could begin to thank her lucky stars that her memory of this link between them had returned, and from here who knew what would come to her next.

But for now, she decided as she stroked her hand down the line of Luc's spine and over his buttocks, she'd relish every second of this reunion.

Luc waited for the racing beat of his heart to slow, for clarity to return to his brain. He'd been so overwhelmed by the power of his response to her he'd barely been able to think, but now he realised he was crushing Belinda. He rolled off her and wrapped his arm about her slender waist, dragging her half over his body as he did so. Her long dark hair spread like a silken cloak across his chest. He inhaled deeply, relishing their comingled scents.

This had turned out far better than he'd antici-pated. He'd expected some flashes of memory, some insights into their past, but he'd never expected her to remember their lovemaking so vividly. He'd been prepared to do whatever it took to get his wife back into his life—the life he'd carved out of nothing, the life he'd vowed would be his one day—and he'd succeeded. It didn't matter to him now if she remembered nothing else. If anything it would probably make life easier for them both.

He listened as Belinda's breathing deepened, as she slid into sleep and he smiled—a grim smile of satisfaction. Their accident had been a short-term derailment of his plan. He was back on track, better than before.

Eight

Belinda stood nervously at Luc's side near the helipad as the Tautara Estate helicopter came up through the valley. After their rediscovery of each other yesterday—a journey that had taken a sultry afternoon of food, wine and making love to complete—she felt almost resentful of this intrusion on their time together. After all, it wasn't as if they'd had a honeymoon—at least not one she remembered, and she still sensed Luc was holding back from her. If not physi-cally, then certainly mentally. She wanted to push past that barrier more than anything. She wanted it all.

Luc still steadfastly refused to disclose any details to her of their past together, or of the accident. The gaps that remained, like yawning black holes in her memory, were increasingly frustrating. She edged closer to her husband and linked her fingers through his. She might not have it all back, she thought, relishing the warm, solid strength of him beside her, but what she did remember was like a gift.

Over breakfast he'd outlined the plans they had for today, that after a light lunch on the patio outside the main living room she and Demi Le Clerc would ride in the chopper to Taupo where they'd do a little shopping while Luc took her fiancé, Hank Walker, to the river for some fly-fishing. As daylight saving hadn't yet finished there'd still be time for Hank to enjoy dangling a few flies for the fish in the river. Tomorrow they'd all travel, again by helicopter, to Hawke's Bay for a vineyard trail ending the day with Demi singing at a concert at one of the vineyard estates.

Under any other circumstances Belinda was certain she'd have enjoyed the coming days entertaining their guests. Under any circumstances other than the fact that in the past twenty four hours she'd rediscovered how hopelessly and passionately she was in love with her husband.

As if he read her thoughts, Luc squeezed gently on her fingers before lifting them to his lips. As the helicopter set down in front of them, Luc turned her away from the buffeting wind, sheltering her with his body. She felt his answering surge of awareness to her proximity, and she deliberately leaned against him, imprinting the evidence of his desire against her. Something she could hold to herself during the next few hours.

"Minx," Luc growled in her ear as the turbines

began to wind down and they heard the door open on the chopper. "How am I supposed to greet our guests like this?"

He flexed against her, leaving her in no doubt that, given the chance, they'd be on their way back to their suite.

"Try not to think about it—" she smiled back "—and try not to think about what I have planned for you tonight."

His pupils flared, their darkness all but consuming the pale green of his eyes.

"I'll deal with you later." While his voice was grim, the belying twinkle in his eyes made her look forward to the night ahead of them with even more urgency than she already possessed. "Now, smile nicely and greet our guests."

Together, hands still linked, they waited for Demi and Hank to come over to them. Belinda didn't miss the hungry rake of Demi's gaze as she kept her heavily made up eyes firmly on Luc, nor did she miss the brief twist of the other woman's lips as her gaze dropped to see their entwined fingers.

Every feminine instinct in Belinda's body went on full alert. If she wasn't mistaken there was a past between these two. A past that went deeper than old friends. She threw a look at Luc but his attention remained on their guests. She'd have given anything for some hint of reassurance from him right now. Some hint that she'd been wrong in her intuitively defensive response to Demi Le Clerc.

The jazz singer was everything Belinda was not. Her short-cropped white-blond hair spiked in an elfin-style cut around her delicate face. Although she was petite, standing no more than about five feet two, and was lightly built, Belinda had the distinct impression that the air of fragility Demi projected was a front for a far, far stronger personality than most people expected.

Belinda pulled her lips back in a smile, hoping against hope itself that Demi Le Clerc would prefer to rest at the Lodge today rather than head out shopping.

Hank Walker was a bit of a surprise. White-haired and stoop-shouldered, he exuded the world-weary air of someone who'd seen it and done it all and was not terribly impressed. Belinda fought down a swell of disquiet. The next few days looked as if they could be hard work.

"Dar-ling!"

Belinda stiffened as Demi launched herself at Luc, forcing him to drop her hand and accept the exuberant embrace from the other woman.

"It's *so* good to see you again. I was thrilled to bits when Hank agreed to include a stop here on our trip. Mind you—" she leaned back a little and gave Luc a lascivious wink "—he did take some convincing."

Belinda fought back a grimace at Demi's saccharine-sweet tone and the allusion she'd made. If she was trying to make Luc jealous, and Belinda suspected that was her intent, it certainly didn't seem to be working. She felt a surge of satisfaction as Luc disengaged Demi's painfully slender arms from around his neck and stepped forward, hand out, to introduce himself to Hank.

The two men appeared to size each other up for a split second before Hank took Luc's hand.

"Welcome to Tautara Estate, Hank. I'm Luc Tanner." He gestured toward Belinda. "Hank, Demi, this is my wife, Belinda."

Was it her imagination or had he placed unnecessary emphasis on the word *wife?* Belinda stepped forward and shook Walker's hand. Demi gave her a swift once-over and a smile that was as fleeting as it was insincere.

"I've heard a lot about you, Luc," Hank drawled with his rich Texas accent. "Read a lot about you, too. Seems there are some rumors about how you got this place."

"There will always be rumors," Luc replied noncommittally.

"So are you saying they're not true? And here I was hoping you were a gambling man after all."

"I've been known to take a gamble, but only when the odds are very firmly on my side."

"Come on, Hank," Demi said in a faux conspiratorial tone, "I told you not to ask him about how he won this place in that poker game."

Belinda fought back a fresh surge of irritation. The woman's words highlighted yet again the gaps in her mind. She should know how Luc came to own Tautara, but it was locked somewhere deep inside. Accepting that, at the moment, Demi Le Clerc knew Luc better than she did herself was a bitter pill to swallow.

Luc gestured toward the house. "Come on inside. Manu has lunch waiting for us on the deck, then we can discuss what we have planned for you both while you're our guests."

"Guests?" Demi hooked one arm through Luc's and the other through that of her fiancé, effectively shutting Belinda completely out. "I think we go back far enough that you should say we're friends—very *good* friends—wouldn't you?"

The woman had all but purred, as she unequivocally staked her claim. Belinda took in a deep breath and forced her shoulders to relax and her hands to unclench before following the trio toward the house. The fact that Demi had in all probability been here before, had, perhaps, even shared Luc's private suite on her previous visits, rankled. As did the thought that she was more familiar with the lodge and its amenities—including its host—than Belinda was.

Well, there was nothing for it but to assert her position as Luc's wife and cohost. As they made their way through the entrance and veered left and through the expansive visitors' lounge room that led to a large deck area she made it her mission to ensure that her "guests" were made to feel as comfortable, and as welcomed, as she could possibly manage. After all, she was the one Luc would sleep with at night.

Manu had clearly done his research well, as the dry martini that Demi obviously preferred, along with the single-malt scotch that was Hank's favourite, were poured as they were ushered into comfortable wicker chairs under the large cantilevered umbrella that shaded this side of the deck. Belinda glided forward to take the drinks from Manu and personally delivered them to their guests with a smile. The glow of approval in Luc's eyes told her she'd done the right thing.

But then, doing the right thing had always been second nature to her. She'd acted as her father's hostess since she'd left school at eighteen—stepping into her mother's shoes as her health had weakened. She'd been so effective in the role she'd almost completely lost her own identity.

It had been frightening how easily she'd been absorbed into her role as effectively as a piece of fine antique furniture in any one of the chain of boutique hotels her father owned and operated. Her gardening, which had started out as a respite from her duties and her father's expectations, had sprung from her desire to break free of her anonymity. Of her need to be someone other than Baxter Wallace's sometime daughter and full-time hostess.

A whisper of something tickled at the back of her mind, triggered by her desire to be her own person, but it disappeared before it could take form.

"Belinda, what can I get you to drink." Manu's voice jolted her from her reverie.

"Just a mineral water, thanks. I think I need to keep my wits about me this afternoon."

Manu gave her a wide grin and said in a low voice that wouldn't reach the others as they sat in their chairs, "I reckon you can hold your own. Don't let that bit of fluff bother you."

"Don't worry, I won't." She smiled back.

It was ridiculous, but suddenly Belinda felt

freer, lighter. As if she had an ally. She leaned against the deck railing and took a sip of her mineral water, enjoying the soft fizz against her tongue and its refreshing path as it travelled down her throat. She could do this. Memory or not.

"I hear you have one of the best herb gardens in the Southern Hemisphere." Hank's deep drawl made Belinda stand upright. "Care to show me around? I'm thinking of getting something along those lines set up at my place. I sure know the cook would be happy if I did."

"I'd be delighted to show you. Luc? Demi? Would you care to join us?" Belinda offered. She was reluctant to leave the other woman in Luc's sole company, but then again, maybe she could give her a dose of her own medicine.

When Demi refused, claiming weariness from travel, Belinda slipped her hand in the crook of Hank's arm and led him away. She didn't miss the twinkle in the older man's grey eyes as they walked back through the house to the elevator that would take them to the lower level and out onto the path leading to the herb garden. Perhaps she hadn't been subtle enough.

"You know you don't have anything to worry about with Demi," Hank said.

"I beg your pardon?"

"Once she realises that whatever she and Luc had before is well and truly gone, she'll back off. It's part of why I agreed to come here. I know she said 'yes' to me on the rebound but, for all her faults, I love her. And she will love me, too. Besides, any fool can see Luc loves you. He can't keep his eyes off you, no matter where you are. Did you catch that glare he gave me as we left? I've seen mountain lions less territorial than he is." He laughed, a rich barrel laugh that forced a smile to Belinda's lips. "Now, show me this garden of yours, and if I like it, you can pay me a visit to design something for me."

By the time they returned to the others, Hank

was trying to convince Belinda to visit his home in Texas to draw up plans for an herb garden on his main residential property. Belinda was laughing at something he'd said as they walked through the large open doors and onto the deck. The look sent her way by Demi was positively wild, and Belinda hoarded the inner victory.

Belinda was surprised when Luc effectively stonewalled Hank's suggestion that they travel up to the States soon so she could choose for herself the best position to put in the garden he was so dead set on having. His deliberate move to change the subject away from her work niggled at the back of her mind, as if he'd done it before. Belinda shook her head slightly. That couldn't be right. Surely he wouldn't stand in her way when it came to doing something she loved so much?

Manu served lunch as they took their seats at the large round table, positioned out of the sun and in such a way as to make the most of the view. When lunch was over, the couples left to change and freshen up, all agreeing to meet at the front entrance in twenty minutes before heading out for their afternoon's activities.

Belinda dallied over reapplying her lipstick; she knew she'd only chew it all off again. Demi had a way about her that constantly kept Belinda on edge, and she wasn't looking forward to their shopping trip one little bit.

Luc's image appeared beside hers in the mirror.

"Are you up for this? No headaches?"

He snaked his hand under her hair and up along the back of her neck. She dropped her head back against his fingers, loving the strength of them as he massaged the tension that had knotted there.

"I'll be okay. After all, we're going shopping, what could possibly go wrong?"

Luc laughed, but his eyes remained serious.

"I'll get Manu to give you a cell phone to use in case you need to come back earlier."

"No, seriously, we'll be fine. *I'll* be fine, even though there's nothing I'd like better than to be home alone with you."

She turned and kissed him on the chin. His fingers tightened at the back of her head, and he tilted her face up toward his before bending slightly to kiss her. Desire flamed, instant and demanding, sending flickers of heat dancing along her nerves. When Luc broke away, she mourned his touch instantly.

"That's for what you did to me before," he growled against her lips, "and for what it's worth, you know I don't want to let you out of my sight, ever. I've suggested a change of plan to Hank, and he's agreed. Instead of coming back here tomorrow night after the concert, they're heading off to one of my other properties near Queenstown. But I'm serious, if you have any doubts about this afternoon, I'll call it off. You can stay here."

"You'd do that for me?" Belinda lifted a hand

to trail her fingers over the scar that marked his jaw. A frisson of something unpleasant tickled at the back of her mind as she touched the smooth skin. She resolutely pushed the sensation away.

"You're my wife. There's no question."

"You say that like it's carved in stone, like *we're* carved in stone."

"Belinda, I hold on to what's mine."

"Was Demi ever yours?"

His face grew rigid under her fingertips. "What has she said to you?"

"She hasn't said a thing, yet. In fact, you might have noticed, she barely acknowledges I exist." Belinda forced a laugh so her comment wouldn't sound too catty. "But you haven't answered my question. Honestly, Luc, while I don't necessarily like it, I can accept that she may have been one of your past lovers, but I'd prefer to be forewarned before I spend the afternoon in her company."

"What Demi and I had was brief. A mistake

she refused to let go of. And that—" he cupped her face with both his hands "—is all I will say on the matter. You have nothing to fear from her. Nothing."

Luc pressed his lips to hers again, as if underscoring what he'd said about Demi Le Clerc being a mistake, as if he could allay Belinda's fears with sheer determination. Helpless to resist him, Belinda opened her lips to his caress, welcomed the invasion of his taste, his tongue, his will.

When Luc made to pull away again she wrapped her arms around his shoulders, refusing to relinquish him. The other woman had made her feel insecure and right now, after the events of the past two days, she needed Luc to be her anchor. Needed him to use more than words to put her mind at ease.

She leaned back against the bathroom vanity, the cool marble imprinting through the silk of her dress in stark contrast to the heat that flamed deep within her body.

"Make love to me, Luc. Here. Now." Her voice was a harsh demand, a plea from her woman's heart, her vulnerability.

In response Luc skimmed his hands down over her shoulders, and lower to fondle her breasts through the fabric of her dress. He bent his head and suckled, through the silk, the moisture of his mouth making the material cling to her aching nipples. She arched her back, thrusting her breasts forward to his mouth, to the pull and release of his lips and tongue.

Her hands fluttered over his shoulders, pushing aside the jacket he wore, then fumbled the buttons of his shirt open. She shoved his shirt down, off his shoulders and free of his arms, then raked her nails lightly across his chest, across the hard flat disks of his nipples. When he groaned in response, the vibration of the sound rippled through, making her nipples tighten even harder.

She pushed the palms of her hands flat, pressing them against the muscles of his chest and dragged them down, over his ribs to the top of his hip, where the shadowed line of his groin began. Getting rid of his belt and the fastenings on his trousers took only a second. Already she could feel his erection pressing against the zipper. She ached to free him, to hold his satin hard length in her hand, to stroke him, feel him, then guide him into the part of her that throbbed for his possession.

His briefs clung to him like a second skin, and she forced herself to slow down as she eased the waistband over his straining flesh and down his legs.

He lifted her to the vanity top, their movement drawing her gaze to the side mirror—their image sent a shocking thrill of excitement through her. There she was, perched on the edge of the rose-tinted marble, her hair in disarray, her eyes bright and gleaming with desire. The fabric of her dress showed dark and wet where Luc had suckled her, her nipples clearly delineated. The skirt was bunched up around her thighs where Luc's hands now slid, his naked torso a direct contrast to her clothed form.

Luc sensed the thrill of desire that rippled through Belinda as she watched their reflection in the side mirror. He lifted her slightly and eased her panties away from her, stepping away from the vee of her legs only long enough to discard the scrap of lace before he settled between her legs again. He was impossibly hard and he needed to be inside her—soon, very soon. She'd become as necessary to him as every breath he took. Necessary in a way that surpassed physical need. He shifted his weight to his good leg, ignoring the nagging pain he'd borne for the better part of the morning—no doubt a result of yesterday's activities. But it had been worth every second of it, as would this time and every time hereafter.

He pulled Belinda forward and she gasped as her backside slid along the cold marble.

He bent his head to the side of her neck, kissing, sucking and gently biting his way down to the curve of her shoulders.

He nestled his hips between her thighs, his erection probing at the hot, honeyed moisture at her entrance. He slid his hands up her arms, to the tiny cap sleeves of her dress and thanked the designer whose deep vee-cut neck and backline had decreed wearing a bra with this dress nigh on impossible. He slid the sleeves of her dress down, trapping her elbows at her sides and exposing the lush fullness of her breasts. The deep rose crests were tight buds, and he drew first one then the other into his mouth. Her shuddering sigh of pleasure was almost his undoing and he lifted her skirt higher, exposing her hips and the curve of her thighs to their view.

Slowly he pushed inside her, fighting the urge to sink himself in her as hard and fast as he could. He watched her expression, saw her eyes glaze and colour spread across her throat and chest. She'd wedged her hands on either side of her hips to keep her balance, using what leverage she had to flex against him, driving him in deeper. She moaned in response, and, now helpless to control his movements, he gave in to the rhythm his body demanded, his hips pumping hard and fast until her cries filled the room and her inner muscles spasmed around him. Pleasure surged through his body in response and he buried his face in her neck, muffling his shout of triumph as his climax ripped through his body and left him trembling against her.

"Now do you believe me?" he growled against her skin. "There is only you in my life. Now and forever."

"Forever," she whispered.

The word bounced softly off the marble of the room, almost as if it was captive, but Belinda remained deaf to its significance.

Nine

They stayed locked together for several minutes, their heartbeats slowly returning to normal, the perspiration on their skin drying. Eventually Luc forced himself to withdraw from her and helped her from the vanity top.

"We're going to have to hurry. Do you want to shower first?"

"There's room for us both, isn't there?" Belinda's tone and flirtatious glance was a far cry from the woman he'd come face-to-face with in her hospital room.

"There is, but not time enough for what we'll end up doing together." He undid the side zipper on Belinda's dress and tugged the garment off her body before turning her toward the shower with a gentle pat on her rear. "Go on."

When they eventually met their guests in the front vestibule, Belinda warded off a sharp glare from Demi. Clearly she was far less than impressed about being kept waiting and didn't hesitate to voice her disapproval.

"Just how long before the shops close? It'll hardly be worth going soon." Her voice was petulant, her eyes cloudy with irritation.

"Don't be ridiculous, honey," Hank placated her. "There'll be plenty for you to see and buy. And why don't you girls stay in Taupo for dinner—it's on me. We'll be fishing until dark. You two may as well stay out and have a bit of fun."

After an hour in Demi's company, Belinda was distinctly weary. It wasn't that Demi was outright rude. But the constant niggles and comparative references to *her* time with Luc, at previous times and during this visit, told Belinda in no uncertain terms that despite what Luc thought, Demi was in no way "over him" just yet. And by the time Demi had turned her nose up yet again at another fashion boutique, Belinda began to despair of being able to keep her temper.

She was on the verge of suggesting they call their driver to take them back to the airfield for the chopper ride home when Demi's eyes suddenly lit on a car rental office.

"Look," she said, pointing. "They hire out luxury cars. Let's ditch the shopping thing and go for a drive around the lake."

"Are you sure you want to do that? It'd take a couple of hours to get around the whole lake, maybe longer," Belinda said.

"Well, let's head north then, what's that place? Oh, yeah, Huka Falls. I heard there was a winery near there."

Before Belinda could stop her, Demi was off across the street and in the office of the rental place. All she could do was sigh and follow her. Demi was pointing to the car she wanted in the catalogue and negotiating pickup from Tautara Estate tomorrow as Belinda walked in the door.

"I thought we could send the chopper back and drive home ourselves after visiting Huka Falls and the winery. The guys won't be back until late, so it's not as if they'll miss us. Give me your phone and I'll let the pilot know."

Surprised, and a little uneasy at Demi's plan, Belinda handed over her cell phone after pulling up the number of their pilot on the screen.

"There." Demi snapped the phone shut. "All settled."

Once the paperwork was complete the two women were taken out the back of the building to where the car had been brought round. Belinda eyed the low slung, blood-red Porsche with some trepidation.

"Are you sure you want this one?" she asked.

"Oh, yes, definitely. Only this one will do. It's almost as flashy as Luc's one was." Demi gave her a piercing look. "You do still drive, don't you?"

"Of course I do," Belinda replied.

At least she thought she did. She'd always had her own car up in Auckland and assumed that that hadn't changed during her time with Luc. But even so, a sense of dread trickled cold and slow down her spine. The fine hairs on her arms stood up against her skin, and she rubbed her arms to ward off the sudden chill that invaded her body.

Demi had already settled herself in the driver's seat and had turned on the ignition before Belinda could force herself forward and into the car. She settled into the deep leather seat and clipped her seat belt on.

"Here." Demi tossed a map on her lap. "You can navigate this section."

Glad for something to do, anything that might distract her from the heavy ball of lead that had settled low in her stomach, Belinda studied the map and gave Demi instructions on how to head out of town. By the time they reached the winery, she'd almost convinced herself that her reaction back at the rental place was just part of the readjustment to normal life. She'd been out of circulation for some time. She'd incurred her head injury in a car accident. No wonder she'd been a little nervous. But Demi was a competent and confident driver, and Belinda had soon relaxed in her seat and enjoyed the countryside as it had swept by them.

The vineyard specialised in a boutique pinot noir, which Belinda really enjoyed. The French barrique-aged wine had a delightful flavour, and even though it was still a young wine she decided to have several cases sent to Tautara Estate to add to Luc's cellar.

It was as they were relaxing over a latte at the adjacent restaurant that Belinda found herself back on full alert.

"I have to say I was surprised to find you and Luc still together when Hank and I arrived," Demi commented as she swept sugar into her coffee and swirled it about with her spoon.

Belinda stiffened in her chair. Her hand arrested midway as she brought her cup to her lips. Without taking a sip of the fragrant coffee, she carefully set the cup back on its saucer.

"Why do you say that?" she replied cautiously.

"Well, because of the accident, of course. I've never understood Luc to be a particularly forgiving man. It just seemed out of character for him, is all." Demi waved a hand airily. "Don't let it bother you. Obviously, it doesn't bother him."

"What doesn't bother him?"

"Well, you were there. Of course you know."

"Actually, no, I don't. I have gaps in my memory. Our accident is one."

For some reason, probably self-preservation, Belinda didn't want to admit to the other massive holes in her mind. She had the distinct feeling that Demi wouldn't hesitate to use the knowledge to her advantage one way or another.

"I've heard that's quite common after a knock on the head. Didn't anyone tell you about it, then?"

"No. The doctors were emphatic that no one tell me what happened. I remember bits here and there, but not the whole picture. Yet."

"Not even Luc? How interesting."

Demi sat back in her chair and gave Belinda an assessing look. Whether she meant it to or not, it made Belinda very uncomfortable, and she wondered what would come next. It was a surprise when Demi did nothing more than turn the conversation back to her upcoming concert tomorrow evening. They lingered over a second coffee, then decided they should head back toward Taupo for a meal and then home. To Belinda's mild relief, Demi automatically slid behind the wheel to drive back.

They took a short detour to the Huka Falls,

where they joined a group of tourists who stood on the over bridge marvelling at the power of the water tumbling at a massive rate beneath their feet. The surge and force of the foaming white water left Belinda feeling a little shaky. Its channelled yet uncontrolled flow was not unlike how she felt in her world at present: guided by the canyon banks, carved out by an ancient eruption, and pushed at an incredible rate to a plummeting fall.

Her fingers gripped the railing in front of her so tight she could feel them burn, but despite that, couldn't bring herself to let go. It was as if the physical act of letting go might actually tumble her over the edge and down through those canyon walls to plunge uncontrollably to an uncertain fate.

As the tourist group moved on to another viewing area, Belinda slowly peeled her hands from the railing.

"I think I'll go and wait by the car, unless

you're ready to head off now?" she said as she started to walk off the bridge.

"Sure, we can head off now. Are you feeling okay? You've gone a bit pale."

Solicitous words from Demi? If Belinda hadn't felt so unbalanced right now she'd have laughed out loud.

"Just a bit of a headache, that's all. Must have been the noise of all that water."

Even as she brushed off the beginnings of another headache, Belinda knew it had nothing to do with the thunderous foaming mass of water. It was as if a dark shadow lingered in the back of her mind. A shadow that demanded acknowledgment. She shook her head slightly, as if she could dislodge the unsettling sensation, and reached in her bag for some painkillers.

She wished Luc was here with her. He would ground her. Make her feel safe and secure.

She would have laughed at herself if she could've summoned the energy. Only days ago she'd refused to leave the hospital with him and now she wanted to be with him more than anything else. She had to hold on to the fact that in another day they'd be alone again. Rediscovering their marriage together.

Her body warmed instantly at the thought, and she hugged the knowledge tightly to her that, while her mind refused to disclose much about their past, her body knew him. In itself that fact gave her a huge amount of security. Their physical union was a connection that could only have been forged, on her part at least, after building a great deal of trust and commitment. As far as she was concerned they couldn't get home soon enough, but she knew she had a duty to perform, as hostess to her guest, and duty was something she took very seriously—no matter the cost.

They chose a hotel near the Taupo waterfront that boasted an award-winning restaurant with picturesque views across the lake. As they swept into the forecourt and a parking valet came forward Belinda was struck by the sense of familiarity the hotel evoked.

The look of shock, hastily disguised by a welcoming smile, on the face of the maître d' momentarily rattled her, but by the time they'd been seated she'd convinced herself she'd been overreacting. The headache that had begun earlier had been effectively dispatched by the tablets she'd taken and she perused her menu with enthusiasm.

"Would you like to see the wine list, madam?" The wine waiter interrupted.

Belinda looked up to Demi who took the proffered list with enthusiasm.

"You go ahead," she said to Demi, "I'll stick with mineral water for now."

"Oh, good. You can drive back to the lodge then. And if you don't remember the way I'll navigate for you!"

Demi's laugh had a harsh edge to it that

Belinda didn't like. She smiled back, but inside she was uncomfortable. By the time their entrees arrived, the other woman had worked her way through the better part of a bottle of wine and was laughing at the slightest thing. She barely touched her main meal, doing little more than push her rack of lamb about her plate.

When the maître d' came by their table to check on their enjoyment of the meals, Belinda was surprised to see the man step away from their table then hesitate before turning back.

"Mrs. Tanner?" he asked.

Belinda started. He knew her by name?

"Yes, I'm Mrs Tanner."

"I just wanted to say how relieved I am to see you're fully recovered from your accident. And your husband—is he well again, too?"

"Yes, thank you. We're both doing fine now." Belinda took a sip of her mineral water before continuing. "May I ask you how you know us?"

The expression on the man's face would

have been laughable if he hadn't looked quite so stricken.

"Mrs Tanner, don't you remember? You had your wedding reception here."

"We did? I'm sorry, there's still so much I don't remember before the accident."

"I'm not surprised. We were all horrified when we heard the crash outside."

"Outside?" Belinda's blood chilled in her veins. "Outside here?"

This was where it had all happened? How could she not have known, not have recognised the place as Demi had driven up into the forecourt?

"Yes, Mrs Tanner, straight after the reception. Are…are you all right, Mrs Tanner? I apologise if I've said anything I shouldn't have. Can I get you anything else?"

"No, no. There's nothing." She forced back the numbing fog of shock to remember her duties as Demi's hostess. "Unless there's something else you'd like?"

Demi just gave her a peculiar look and shook her head.

"Well, if you don't mind I think we'll settle the bill and head back to Tautara." Belinda tried to smile but her lips felt wooden, her face as if it was set in stone.

As they waited in the front portico of the hotel for the parking valet to bring the car around, the cell phone Manu had given her earlier started to trill. She'd no sooner flipped it open when she could hear Luc's baritone.

"Where are you? Why did you send the chopper back?"

"Luc! How was the fishing?"

"Fine. We've just come back to the house. Where are you?"

"We're at—" Belinda looked around and spied the name of the hotel in gold lettering over the front door. She told him the name only to be met with stony silence. "Luc? Are you still there?"

"Why are you there?"

"We stopped here for dinner. Demi thought it would be a good place." She took a deep breath. "I didn't know it was where we had our reception or…or the accident."

"Are you okay? You sound shaky."

Just then the valet drove their rental car onto the forecourt and swung it to a halt in front of the two women.

"Here, give me that." Demi stepped forward and took the cell phone from Belinda's suddenly nerveless fingers. "Luc, it's Demi. Look, our car's just been brought round so we're on our way back."

Belinda heard Luc's voice resonate through the phone's tiny speaker.

"Car? What car?"

"The car I hired when we sent the helicopter back. You should see it. It's a Porsche Carrera, a lot like your old one, really."

"Stay there, I'll come and get you."

"Get us? Don't be silly. We'll be fine. We should be back in about half an hour to forty minutes."

"Demi—"

Demi snapped the phone closed and handed it back to Belinda with a smile.

"Men. They're always trying to order us women about. It has its uses, but Luc always did overdo it. Come on, let's head back."

She slipped into the passenger seat and settled herself, giving the valet a smile as he closed her door. Belinda had no option but to get behind the wheel of the low-slung sports car.

Demi gave her a strange, almost challenging look as she clipped her seat belt.

"You have driven a stick shift before, haven't you?"

"Yes, of course. But it was ages ago."

Belinda swallowed against the bile that suddenly rose in her throat as she settled one hand on the steering wheel and rested the other on the gearshift. Her skin had turned cold and clammy and she wanted nothing better right now than to pull at her clothing, which suddenly stuck to her body as if she was bathed in perspiration. She could do this. She'd driven a car for years. But then, why was she suddenly, sickeningly, filled with dread?

She put in the clutch and selected first gear when the blinding shaft of pain hit behind her eyes. Her foot slid off the pedal and the car lurched away from the portico to stall ignominiously on the drive. A small frightened cry fought past her tightly pressed-together lips.

Belinda closed her eyes tight and pressed the heels of her palms against them as visceral visual memories blasted past the blocks of her mind. Pictures of her behind the wheel of a car similar to this one, except its paintwork was as dark as midnight—the lights of the forecourt gleaming on its pristine surface.

An overwhelming sense of fear mixed with anger and, yes, betrayal, made her breathing tighten in her chest. She'd been alone in the car and in the driver's seat—her wedding dress, a foam of white organza in the leg bay. Tears blinded her eyes as she'd put the car in gear and applied her foot vigorously to the accelerator. Everything in her focused on only one thing— to get away.

Then suddenly, in front of her, Luc tore across her path. And she was too late. Too late to stop.

She relived again the horrified sob that wrenched from her throat as she'd swerved, the car slewing to the left as she tried unsuccessfully to avoid him. Then the terror as his body crumpled to the gravelled driveway before her as her ears were filled with a deafening crunch of metal and glass and everything went mercifully black.

"What the hell do you think you were doing?" Luc's furious voice penetrated the darkness, followed immediately by Hank's protestation.

"Now quieten down, boy. It's not Demi's fault.

Your wife shouldn't have been behind the wheel of that car, and you know it."

Belinda fought to raise her eyelids as the voices swirled around her.

"Yes, I do know it. That's precisely why I'd arranged the helicopter and a driver for them in Taupo. Whose idea was it to hire the Porsche?"

"Mine, it was mine." Demi's voice was defensive. "Someone had to do something. You weren't prepared to do anything about her memory loss."

"On instructions from her medical team. Instructions I made clear to you. You had no right to do what you did."

"I thought she was faking it. That's why I did it. For God's sake, Luc, she nearly killed you, and you still brought her home!"

"That was my choice to make. She's my wife."

Belinda sensed a tension between Luc and Demi that threatened to boil over into a full-blown conflagration. She had to stop it, stop them.

"Luc?" Her voice was thready.

He was at her side immediately, his strong arm a secure comfort as it snaked around her shoulders, helping her as she struggled upright.

"What's going on? Where are we?"

Belinda looked around the room. Nothing was familiar to her.

"We're at the hospital, but I'm taking you home. You don't need to stay here."

"Please, take me home now."

Luc had people move with a swiftness that saw them settled back at Tautara within the hour. She'd remained silent for the journey in the chopper and hadn't protested when Luc had suggested she go straight to bed when they got back to the house.

"Will you be all right for a few minutes? There's something I need to sort out, but I'll be straight back."

With a weary sigh Belinda leaned against the pillows he'd insisted on propping behind her. "Sure. I'm not going anywhere right now."

As soon as he was gone, she closed her eyes and willed sleep to claim her. Anything would be easier than acknowledging the dreadful memories that now scarred her consciousness.

She'd been the source of the accident that had caused Luc's injuries. She'd been the one to leave him permanently scarred and with a limp he had to live with for the rest of his life. Tears seeped out from beneath her closed lids, and her throat choked up with the enormity of what she'd done. No wonder she hadn't wanted to remember something so dreadful.

But why had it happened? Why had she been behind the wheel of his car? Even now she could recall how desperate she'd felt, how desolate and determined she'd been to get away from what was supposed to have been the happiest day of her life. What could possibly have happened that was so bad that it had made her want to run away from the man she'd just pledged her love to in marriage?

Ten

Dimly, she became aware of the sound of Luc's helicopter spooling up then taking off, the noise of the engine and rotors diminishing as it flew away from the property.

A soft click of the bedroom door was the only warning she had that he was back. The bed depressed as he sat down beside her. She could feel his eyes boring into her, but she couldn't bring herself to face him. How did you look into the eyes of the man you loved more than life itself and admit you'd nearly killed him? Worse, you didn't even know why.

His body shifted on the mattress, then a long, cool finger traced the path of the tears on her cheeks.

"Tears, Belinda? Why?"

She kept her eyes firmly closed and her lips equally so. She couldn't tell him she remembered. Not this. Anything but this. Inside she felt as if her heart was being splintered apart into a thousand shards. Shards that turned inward and struck her anew with the pain of what she now remembered so vividly. Remembered and fervently wished she could shove back into the dark and never know again.

The gentle pressure of his lips on hers was her undoing. She wrenched her head away and pushed her hands against his chest, trying to put some distance between them.

"No, don't," she begged.

"Why not?" His voice held a steely note that demanded an answer. One she was sure he would not be happy to hear.

"Because of what I did."

"What you did? Tell me. What do you remember?"

"I…I nearly killed you. How can you want me with you when I ran you down in your own car?"

"It was an accident."

"Was it? How do you know that? You have to tell me the truth of what happened. Why was I driving your car? Why weren't you in it with me? Why did you bring me back here when you must hate what I did to you—must hate me!"

Her voice had grown in strength and volume as she peppered him with questions. Shudders racked her body over and over. Yet still he didn't turn away from her. Instead he grabbed her hands with his and pulled her forward into his arms, holding her against his chest as she sobbed out her fear and frustration.

"I should never have sent you out with that woman for the whole afternoon. I knew she couldn't be trusted."

* * *

Luc cursed under his breath. He'd underesti-
mated Demi, and it would cost him dearly. If
Belinda remembered too much too soon, it could
set his plans awry. Damn, but he could wring
Demi's neck. Hank had obviously sensed the
latent anger in him. He'd accepted Luc's suggestion that they leave immediately for Napier,
staying at the home of one of Luc's business as-
sociates prior to the concert tomorrow night.

He stroked his fingers through Belinda's hair
again and again until her sobs began to subside
and the shudders that racked her body stilled.
Gently he set her away from him, pushing her
back against the pillows again. He studied her
pale face and wished undone the damage that
had been wrought today.

What would she remember next? Would she
remember it all, now that large chunks of what
had happened were coming back to her? Whether
she did or she didn't, didn't matter. She would
never leave him again, he'd made certain of that.

"How can you even bear to look at me?"

"Look at you? Why wouldn't I want to look at you? Even if you weren't my wife, you're a beautiful woman. Looking at you, knowing you're mine, gives me the utmost pleasure."

He could see his answer confused her. What had she expected, he wondered. A declaration of undying love? He clenched his teeth together. He didn't do emotion. She'd remember that again soon. How would she react? Would it be like last time, the fight-or-flight reflex taking over? Whatever she did, he had the means to prevent her from running again.

"Luc, I nearly killed you. I know I was trying to get away from you and that you tried to stop me. Why?"

"Why did I try to stop you? That's simple. We'd just gotten married. You heard something that upset you and you tried to run away. I had to stop you. I couldn't let you hurt yourself."

"Instead I hurt you. Was it deliberate?"

Luc had asked himself the very same question

but had come to the conclusion that it had been a complete and utter accident. Her unfamiliarity with the six-speed gearbox of the powerful sports car, and her very nature, lent weight to that deduction. Convincing the police not to lay charges against his unconscious wife while he'd been trapped in a hospital bed had been easier said than done.

"No, of course it wasn't deliberate. You were upset, you made a misjudgment. I should never have stepped in front of the car. It was as much my fault as it was yours. Believe me, if you had deliberately tried to run me down, the police would have been at the hospital waiting for the moment you came out of your coma so they could arrest and charge you."

He saw her shoulders drop slightly as she began to relax.

"Then why? What was I doing, what was I thinking? It was our wedding day. We should have been leaving our reception together."

"I can't tell you what you were thinking, Belinda." That much at least was true. He'd had no idea that she would react the way she had, when she'd learned the truth behind their marriage. "But I know if I had to do the same thing again to stop you from leaving me and hurting yourself, I would."

"Even if it meant I'd end up hurting you?"

She looked so confused, so fragile, both mentally and physically as she lay in their bed. Luc took one of her hands in his and lifted it to his lips to press a kiss inside her wrist.

"Even then."

He saw the flare of heat in her eyes at his caress, felt his own answering response. He stroked his tongue gently across the fluttering pulse beneath the pale skin of the inside of her wrist.

"Oh, Luc. How can you still want me after what I did?"

"I will always want you. From the first time I saw you I wanted you. I will never let you go. Never."

He leaned forward and caught her lips in a kiss designed to leave her in no doubt of his intentions, in no doubt of his desire to possess and keep her. She responded like someone who'd been thrown a lifeline in a turbulent sea, her arms linking around his neck and holding him to her as if she was afraid he'd disappear if she let go.

The sweep of her tongue across his lower lip sent a jolt of need through his body. Instantly he wanted her with a desperation he had never thought to feel again. A desperation born of fear of losing her. The fear itself was ridiculous. She would never, could never, leave him again. He knew that as well as he knew each exquisite line of her body. But a small voice deep inside him urged him to admit to wanting more, to needing more than simple possession.

Luc pushed aside the thought with the same ruthless urgency as he cast away his clothing, then divested Belinda of the robe she'd wearily drawn over her body after undressing earlier.

His hands shook as he caressed her shoulders and trailed his fingers across the sweep of her collarbone then lower to test the weight and fullness of her breasts.

When she pressed against his hands, silently begging for a harder touch, he obliged—squeezing the globes of flesh with a firmness that saw her nipples harden into tight beads of deepest rose. He bent his head to take the crest of one breast between his teeth, his tongue flicking against its rigid point until she cried out with pleasure, her nails raking his shoulders.

He replaced his tongue with his fingers, pulling and drawing at her nipples as she squirmed against him. He could smell her desire on the air around them and he knew he had to taste her—to drive her to peak after peak of pleasure. To imprint that pleasure that only he could give her on her mind and to effectively obliterate her fears and insecurities. To affirm her place in his life, in his bed.

Her skin quivered as he traced his tongue around her belly button, dipping into its centre and probing the perfect indentation again and again in a teasing mimic of what he planned to do next. When he trailed his tongue lower, to the curve of her inner thigh, her legs fell open, giving him free rein to do with her whatever he wanted. And he wanted. Wanted her so deeply he knew he would never let her go.

He nuzzled against the moist curls at the apex of her thighs, sliding his hands beneath her buttocks, tilting her toward him, opening her further so he had clear and unlimited access.

He dipped his tongue to her centre, stroking deeply, allowing his teeth to graze the shiny nub of flesh that was the key to her release.

She writhed against him, her breath coming in quick pants. His own body burned in response, urging him to rise above her and surge into her—to take him over that edge and into the abyss where only pleasure mattered. Where the past no longer existed. But with a discipline learned from a life of hardship and denial, he held himself back. His first priority was Belinda. First and always.

Beneath his onslaught her body tautened, and he knew, with a rising sense of satisfaction, she was close to orgasm. He eased one finger inside her, smiling as her inner muscles clenched around him instantly. He stroked her deep inside, alternating flicks of his tongue across her swollen bud with the pressure of his finger until her hips rose off the bed and her body bowed and shook as the waves of her climax pounded through her.

Her cheeks were streaked with tears, her eyes glazed as he slid up over her body and positioned himself at her entrance.

Belinda was boneless, floating on a sea of pleasure such as she'd never known before, and yet, as she felt the weight of Luc's body on hers, felt the blunt pressure of his erection probing her core, she was revitalised. She wanted him more than she ever had before. Needed him more. All of him, in every way. She needed to know, more than anything in her life, that the terrible wrong she'd done him was forgiven.

She opened her body to him, lifting her hips and wrapping her legs around his waist. She caught his face between her hands and kissed him, the taste of her own desire on his lips unusual and yet enticing at the same time. As he eased his length inside her body she suckled on his tongue and rocked against him, drawing him deeper within her until she thought she could take no more.

A jolt of ecstasy shot from deep within her, radiating out through her limbs and making her cry out with the sensation, relinquishing his tongue, his mouth, as her head dropped back against the pillows. Pressure built within her body again, faster than before, harder than before, and she moved in rhythm with him as he drove into her with increasing tempo.

She stroked her hands across his chest, over his shoulders and down his back—his muscles marble hard with tension beneath her touch. Lower and lower she trailed her finger tips until she traced the cleft of his buttocks, felt the clench and release of sinew and power beneath her caress.

And then, with a raw shout, he drove deeper than before, his entire body taut as he fought to stave off his climax for just a moment longer. Ripples of pleasure radiated through her in ever-increasing waves until she gave herself over to the sensations. As she did so, felt his body melt into her own, his hips thrusting, straining, as he finally gave in and allowed gratification to dominate him once more.

Tiny pulses of satisfaction, like tiny electric shocks, vibrated through her body as they lay entwined on the bedcovers. Now that Luc's sensual onslaught had reached an end, she allowed herself to think again about what had happened today. About the shock of remembering what and who had caused his terrible injuries.

Luc's breathing deepened as he lay beside her, his face nestled in the curve of her neck. Belinda stroked her hand down his body, down to his hip and along the path of his scar as it trailed down his thigh.

"I'm sorry," she whispered into his hair. "I'm sorry I hurt you."

"It's in the past," he said, his voice deep and thick with the edges of slumber. "We'll talk more tomorrow. Now, sleep."

"Luc?"

"Hmmm?"

"I love you."

In response his arms closed around her tight, drawing her along the length of his body where she knew she belonged. He pressed his lips against her throat.

"I know." His words were a deep rumble against her skin.

Belinda held her breath, waiting for more. Waiting for him to tell her he loved her, too, but she waited in vain as his body relaxed more deeply into hers and his breathing became more measured, indicating he had fallen deeply asleep.

She stared into the darkness, thoughts and fears pounding at her mind. Did he love her, too, or had she destroyed that when she'd almost destroyed him? That he wanted her, desired her, was obvious. But physical love was only one part of a relationship. What of the rest? Of the melding of minds, the reciprocal emotional bond that came from a union between life mates?

Despite the heat of Luc's body as he slumbered beside her, she felt a chill ripple through her soul. Something hovered on the shadowed periphery of her consciousness, and she fought unsuccessfully to grasp it with her mind even as sleep finally claimed her.

* * *

Luc's eyes flicked open, straining to see in the darkened room, the words Belinda had uttered echoing in his mind. Instead of the triumph he'd anticipated, he was consumed with an aching need to respond in kind. But he knew from bitter experience that could only lead to pain. Hadn't his mother's last words been of love for his father—the man who'd ended up destroying them both? No, better that he cap his feelings. Better that Belinda's love not be returned.

Belinda woke the next morning surprisingly rested, and when Luc suggested they have a swim before breakfast she accepted his idea eagerly. The indoor solar-heated pool with its roll-away ceiling, open today to make the most of the late summer sunshine, looked inviting. Luc dived in, cutting cleanly through the water, and for a moment Belinda merely revelled in the beauty of his body as he swam one length after another.

In the water there was no sign of the weakness in his leg, no sign of the limp that marked him as flawed. She knew how much it bothered him to carry such a defect, and it scored her deeply to know she was responsible for that. Yet he'd forgiven her, he'd reiterated that again today when they'd changed for their swim, telling her to leave the past firmly in the past where it belonged.

"Aren't you coming in?" Luc's head, dark and sleek with water popped up in front of her.

"Sure I am."

"What's holding you back, then?"

Belinda let her eyes roam over the corded muscles in his neck, the breadth of his powerful shoulders and chest where they were exposed, slightly out of the water.

"Just enjoying the view, that's all." She injected a teasing note in her voice. Anything was better than admitting the truth that she was even more racked with guilt this morning than she had been last night.

The reality of the long-term effects of his injury sat heavily on her shoulders. The requirements of his position as a host and guide to their overseas guests demanded a certain level of fitness. A fitness that had been sorely damaged due to her actions.

She shook her head slightly to free herself of the lingering sense of dread that still clung on the fringes of her mind.

"I'll race you to the other end," she challenged, diving over his head and neatly into the water.

She struck out firmly across the water as soon as she broke the surface, a thrill of excitement surging through her as she felt his presence close behind. She reached the opposite side, muscles burning at the unaccustomed exercise, a split second before strong fingers wrapped around her ankle and tugged her under. Beneath the water's surface she allowed herself to sink into his waiting arms, her body leaping to life the instant her flesh joined with his.

She could feel the curve of his lips as they kissed beneath the water, sensed the power in his legs as he kicked them back up toward the surface.

"You cheated," he growled against her mouth. "I should punish you for that."

"And if I concede?" She nipped at his lips.

"Then you get to punish me."

"Would that be before or after breakfast?" she teased.

Luc laughed, the sound echoing through the rafters of the pool house and setting light to a deep sense of joy inside Belinda. In the days since they'd come to Tautara, come home, she hadn't heard him give vent to unabashed humor like that. To know she'd been the one to draw it from him made her feel incredibly special. And it made her all the more determined to make him happy like that again and again.

Once out of the pool, they dried each other off, then wrapped themselves in robes. Belinda was fully prepared to forgo breakfast by the time she'd towelled away the moisture from Luc's perfectly proportioned body and, judging by the reaction of one of those proportions, he was, too. Then Manu called through on the intercom to let them know breakfast was ready on the upper deck of the house.

She paused a moment, as they were about to leave the pool house, to wriggle out of her wet bikini bottoms and undo the ties of her top and pull it away from her body.

"What are you doing?" Luc asked, his eyes burning bright with a look she'd come to recognise.

Belinda felt an answering pull at her womb as she chose her words.

"I can't stand wet swimwear against my skin," she said as casually as she could as she walked through the door Luc held open for her.

"And I'm supposed to keep my mind and my hands on breakfast knowing you're naked beneath that robe?"

"Think of it as your punishment."

She smiled and flicked the lapel of his robe to emphasise her point.

"Ah." Luc slid a hand inside the thick toweling to cup her breast, his thumb lightly stroking her nipple. "But I didn't hear you concede."

Her answer caught on the breath that hitched in her throat as, with his body, he pinned her back against the wall. His hair-roughened thigh slid between her legs to rub against her. The contrast of the sudden chill of his damp swim trunks against her heated core made her gasp out loud, the sound swiftly muffled by Luc's lips on hers as he took her mouth in a hungry kiss. He flexed his hips against her, rubbing the ridge of his arousal across her, sending her into an instant flare of burning need.

"Still can't stand wet swimwear against your skin?" he whispered into the shell of her ear.

Luc pulled away from her and straightened her robe before taking her hand and leading her back upstairs to the deck. Belinda could barely think, let alone speak. In a split second he'd turned her on so much she'd have thrown care and propriety to the wind and let him take her against the glass-lined pool house wall. Visible for any of the staff to see as they made their way around the property.

Her wholehearted absorption in him and in everything he aroused in her was daunting. No wonder she'd agreed to marry him. Even in these few short days, with the limited memories she'd regained, he'd become the centre of her world.

So why, then, had she been trying to run away?

Eleven

"**W**hat would you like to do today?" Luc asked as he sliced a mushroom on his plate. "I have some work to attend to this morning, but we can do whatever you like for the rest of the day."

"If you're going to work, I'll spend some time in the garden. I've missed getting my hands dirty." She smiled.

"You don't need to get your hands dirty. We have staff for that."

"But, Luc, it's something I enjoy, something I love."

Luc reached across the table and took one of her hands in his. Sunlight caught the blue diamond of her engagement ring, refracting light across the white linen tablecloth like blue fire. For all they were dining al fresco, everything was still five-star. Whatever they promised their clientele, it was obvious that this was a way of life Luc lived, as well. He offered perfection and expected it in return.

He rubbed her fingers between his. "Just make sure you wear gloves. You don't want to ruin your beautiful hands."

There was a note in his voice that set Belinda's spine straight, made her feel prickly and defensive. She pushed the thought aside. He only cared for her welfare, she told herself.

"Sure, if it'll make you happy."

"Having you as my wife makes me happy," he replied, lifting her fingers to his lips and licking lightly between the knuckles.

Again, that frisson of discomfort trickled

down her back, raising a question in her mind. Was it having *her,* or having her as *his wife* that made him happy? The question bothered her and she absentmindedly spread marmalade over her toast as she tried to figure out why.

She felt as if she'd truly come home when she entered this part of the gardens. To one side of the shade house stood a shed, lined with shelves filled with terra-cotta pots of all sizes and shapes and with bags of potting mix stacked against one wall. Just outside the shed a pink-veined marble replica of Venus de Milo stood in lonely splendor.

Belinda trailed her hand along the line of the statue's shoulder. She could sympathise with Aphrodite on this score, she thought, as her hand dropped past where the statue's right arm would have finished. It seemed as if nothing was complete in her world right now, either— at least not in her memory. There were still vast tracts of emptiness, gaps splintered by sudden glimpses of the past.

She sighed and looked around her. So much here was familiar, comforting in a way. It would be good to be busy doing something she loved again.

Much later that morning Manu brought her a phone as she worked on repotting some cuttings she'd found in an overgrown mass in a shade house around the side of the herb garden. Obviously, she'd been experimenting with cuttings and grafting prior to their marriage. Those that had taken were strong and healthy, if not a little unruly. Unfortunately, just as many plants had shrivelled up and died. She hoped that wasn't symbolic.

Manu stepped through the doorway with a big smile, and Belinda dusted off her hands on her jeans, having long since discarded the unwieldy gardening gloves she'd donned purely because Luc had requested it.

"Enjoying yourself?" Manu asked, with a twinkle in his deep-set brown eyes.

Laughter bubbled from her throat. "Oh, yes! Definitely."

"That's good. We've missed your smiles around here, you know. Here—" he passed her the cordless phone "—there's a call for you from Auckland. Someone at Pounamu Productions."

"Really, what on earth could they want?"

"Take it and see."

Belinda inspected her hands quickly before accepting the cordless phone and put the phone to her ear.

"Hello? This is Belinda Wal—Tanner." She grimaced comically at Manu at her slip. She'd automatically gone to use her maiden name. Mind you, that wasn't so surprising considering that she still couldn't even remember her wedding.

"Belinda, still not used to being a married woman, eh? Look, it's Jane Sinclair from Pounamu Productions. Do you remember that series we were discussing before your wedding, the half hour per week gardening show? The money men have given us the go-ahead and the powers-that-be love the stills we took of you in your family gardens. They think you're a natural for the job, and the fact you're so gorgeous will widen our audience appeal. When can you come up to Auckland to discuss it further?"

Belinda absorbed Jane's words in stunned silence. Television series? Weekly gardening show? How on earth was she supposed to tell Jane she had absolutely no idea what she was talking about. Disregarding Belinda's lack of response Jane carried on talking about plans for the series, production schedules and all manner of things.

"So, how about next week? Does that suit?" she finished.

"Look, I'll need to get back to you to confirm, but that should be fine," Belinda hedged. "Give me your number."

She scrabbled around on her workbench. She

knew she'd seen a marker pen somewhere. A pen and paper appeared in front of her and she flung Manu a grateful look as she rapidly copied down Jane's contact details. By the time she pressed the off button on the phone, she felt as if she'd run a marathon. She looked at Manu in puzzlement, briefly outlining the call.

"Do you know what she was talking about?"

His normally open face assumed a set expression, his eyes giving nothing away. "You'll have to talk to Luc about that. He's still in his office. Do you want me to call him for you?"

"No, that's okay. No need to disturb him. I'll see him at lunchtime. We can talk about it then."

"No worries." He turned to leave, then hesitated in the doorway. "How do you feel about it? That's some opportunity you have there."

"Yeah, it is." She sank onto a stool behind her and met his gaze full-on. "I would have jumped at this opportunity before, I just know it, but something's telling me not to. That it's not right." She shook her head. "I don't know. Seems life would be a whole lot easier if I could just remember everything."

"Ah, well, as my *tipuna* would say, don't trouble trouble until trouble troubles you. Sometimes it's just as well to leave well enough alone."

"Your grandmother was a wise woman. Thanks, Manu."

As he left the shade house, she pondered his words, and the almost cautionary tone in which he'd delivered them. Was it best for her not to keep pushing to remember? She doubted that very much. If her marriage was going to be fulfilling, she had to be able to come to it a whole woman with a whole mind, not, she smiled to herself, one with holes in her mind.

"What's so funny?"

Luc's voice from the doorway made her start.

"Manu said you were still working." She reached up and kissed the cleft in his chin. "Is it time for lunch already?"

Luc picked up her hands in his and gave her a stern look. "Whether it's lunchtime or not, I think it's time you took a break. Look at you."

Belinda ruefully examined her hands. "They'll scrub up okay. Besides, it's not as if I'm on show or anything, is it?" She strived to keep her tone light, but the command in Luc's voice was unmistakeable—and she didn't like it one bit.

"I wouldn't call it 'on show,' exactly, but we're expecting more guests in the next few days and will have near full capacity over the next six weeks. You know I need you by my side, looking beautiful."

Belinda forced a laugh. "You make me sound like an ornament. Surely I'm more important than just that."

"Endlessly." Luc scooped one arm around Belinda's waist and pulled her to him. "You're the most important thing in my world. Is it any wonder I just want to keep you near me as much as I can?"

She was saved from responding as Luc bent his head and kissed her, his tongue stroking her lower lip lightly, coaxing her to open her mouth and allow him entry. Her body flamed to instant aching life. It seemed she couldn't get enough of him—of his taste, his strength—all of him. Whether it had been his intention to thoroughly distract her or not, it worked supremely well and by the time Luc coaxed her from her potting mix and pots, she was looking forward to the afternoon they were to spend together.

Back up in their suite she took a quick shower and changed into clean jeans and a long-sleeved white linen blouse over a soft blue silk chemise. Luc hadn't told her exactly what they'd be doing but had intimated she'd need to dress casual and to bear in mind protection from the sun.

As she picked up her gardening clothes to put them in the laundry hamper, a slip of paper poked out from a pocket. She snagged it between her fingers, looking at the name and number she'd scrawled so hurriedly. She thought about Luc's forewarning that they'd be a full house with guests in the next week. She'd have to check with him when would be a good time to go to Auckland for her meetings.

She stroked the paper between her fingers, staring at the name—willing something, anything, to spring into her mind about the proposed television series. Suddenly a picture burst in her mind, of Jane Sinclair in the gardens at Baxter Wallace's Devonport-based boutique hotel for a wedding. The woman had enthused for ages about the beauty of the old roses, the arbours, the scented plantings Belinda had bordered the property with. When she'd heard Belinda was responsible for that and many of the other Wallace hotel-chain gardens she'd simply gushed with ideas.

Belinda had been hugely excited. Working with her father over the past few years—acting as his right hand as her mother had begun to find the task increasingly wearying—had always been more of a duty than a pleasure. While she did it, as she did everything, with the utmost confidence and competence, gardens were where her heart lay. She loved every part of it. The planning, selecting the plantings, overseeing the work—every stage had its rewards right through to completion.

She'd worked for years, albeit part-time, trying to build a portfolio from which to grow her fledgling design business and now, finally, she was being given the platform from which to launch—to soar and fly and achieve her dreams.

Belinda shoved the small sheet of paper into the pocket of her jeans and rushed through to the dining room where Luc waited for her. She couldn't wait to tell him about Jane's call—and better yet, that she remembered the reasons why.

It didn't for a minute occur to her that he'd object.

"It's impossible. Give me the Sinclair

woman's number and I'll let her know you won't be participating."

Belinda dropped her fork to her plate with a clatter.

"I beg your pardon?" She was incredulous. "Why ever not?"

"I told you. I need you here. This is our livelihood. Our guests expect a host and a hostess, with all the trimmings. It's what you do best, so let's hear no more of this television show."

"What I do best? But, Luc, this is an opportunity I can't turn away. Just think of the commissions I could get for doing gardens like our herb garden. Even Hank wants me to design something for him."

Across the intimately set table in their dining room, Luc stilled. "Hank Walker? No."

"Okay, I agree that working for him would be difficult with Demi and everything. Still, a trip to Texas would've been fun, wouldn't it?"

"That trip is never going to happen, just like

you hosting this TV show isn't going to happen, either."

Belinda's spine stiffened as she looked at him. Had he gone completely mad?

"What do you mean, never?"

"Your place is here. By my side."

"By your side? But what of my work, Luc. I have a business to rebuild."

"No, you don't."

Luc watched Belinda carefully from across the table. It had been only a matter of time. His greatest fears were coming to life as her memory returned. He could feel himself losing her already, and the sensation struck dread deep into his heart. Was it so wrong to want to keep her here, by his side? He pushed himself to his feet and walked around to her. He reached for her hand, clenched in a tight fist in her lap, and pulled her up against him. Her eyes looked more grey than blue—cold, defensive—as if he'd suddenly grown horns from his forehead. And maybe to all intents and purposes he had— because the devil would take him before he'd let her go. Under his gaze she paled, her lips fading to the palest of pink, her cheeks totally devoid of colour.

He bent his head to kiss her, to kiss away the anger and fear that reverberated from her like a tangible force, but she turned her head away. Damn, he didn't like the way this was heading, or the sudden sensation of vulnerability that sliced through him.

"We've had this conversation before, haven't we?"

She brushed a hand across her forehead, rubbing across the line of her brow as if to coax something from her mind. Luc remained silent, watchful. He recognised the signs now. She was getting a headache, a precursor to her remembering something that distressed her and that invariably led to a loss of consciousness. He tightened his hold on her, only to have her pull free and step away from the safety of his arms.

Lord, it was only yesterday that she'd remembered the accident. The memories were coming thicker and faster than before. And he, damnably, had no control over them.

Sudden awareness shot through her features.

"We have." Her voice rose, a thread of anger running like a vein of steel through it. "It was straight after the wedding."

"Go on," he said, fighting to keep his voice level. Fighting back the words of denial that he knew were a lie.

She blinked a few times in quick succession, her brow furrowing as she appeared to sort through the vagaries of her mind. When she lifted her head, her eyes were bright with anger and something else he couldn't immediately identify.

Pain.

It was pain. Pure and simple and wrenching in its presence. Emotional pain of a type he'd never permitted himself to acknowledge. Yet seeing Belinda so stricken sent a piercing arrow of empathy deep inside to the dark place he kept hidden from everyone. Even himself.

Luc reached for her, again but Belinda was quicker. She stepped out of his reach, shaking her head, her voice low.

"Don't touch me."

"Belinda, stop."

"Stop? Stop what, Luc? Stop remembering that you only married me because I was the best applicant for the job? Stop remembering that you deliberately wooed me here to Tautara and then wooed me into your bed?" She slammed her hand on the table beside them, making the plates and cutlery jump. A glass toppled and rolled off the edge and onto the tiled dining-room floor, shattering into pieces. "Tell me, am I on track? Is there anything in particular I might have left out?"

She stared at him, tears welling in her eyes.

Inside he felt as if a tenuous link had begun to break apart.

"I never lied to you, Belinda."

"No, you didn't. And you never loved me, either."

The tears finally spilled over her lower lashes, tracking in lines of silver down her cheeks.

"And that's a crime? Love is for fools. What we have is—"

"What we had." She interrupted him with a finality in her voice that froze him where he stood.

"Had?"

"You don't expect me to stay here now I know, do you? I was leaving you the night of the accident. The night we were supposed to be celebrating our marriage. How could you keep that from me and expect me never to remember—never to want to leave you again? I hate you for what you did to me, what you've done to me now."

She spun on her heel and headed for the door.

"Stop. Where do you think you're going?" he demanded, his hands knotted into fists of frustration at his side. No matter what the provocation he would not let go of his anger. He was not like his father, but he would not let Belinda go. Not when she was the centre of his world. He could not.

"I'm leaving. Leaving Tautara and leaving you. You can't stop me."

Her hand was on the doorknob, turning the polished brass and releasing the catch.

"You're right. I can't stop you." He struggled to inject the right note of nonchalance in his tone. As he'd hoped she hesitated and turned at his words.

"Is this some kind of trick?"

"Trick? No, I'm not into games. Never have been." There'd been no games in his childhood. Life had been serious from the get-go, deathly so. He slowly walked toward his wife; noted the way her fingers tightened nervously on the doorknob. "I certainly can't stop you leaving, but you might like to consider the effect of your doing so on your parents."

"On my parents? They wouldn't want me to stay in this…this…'relationship' any longer than I have already. If Dad had any idea of how cold-bloodedly you married me, he'd be helping me out this door as fast as he could."

"Are you so certain of that? Perhaps you should speak to your father before you leave. Make sure you'll be welcome home."

"Why wouldn't I be? I'm their youngest child. I've worked at my father's side for years, helped my mother in every way I can. Of course I'd be welcome home." Twin spots of colour appeared in her cheeks, bright in the porcelain pale of her skin.

"Then perhaps he won't mind so much when I call in my loan. Of course, it'll mean that your mother will have to cease the treatment she's just started in America, and your father's hotels, well, they'll no doubt be sold to defray some of those costs. It's even possible your sisters' husbands will lose their positions managing their hotels. Maybe they'll find other work to sustain the lifestyles they're all accustomed to, maybe not. But it'll all be worth it in the name of love, won't it?"

He stepped past her and opened the door of their suite. "You're free to go anytime you want. Just be sure that you can live with the consequences."

Twelve

Belinda sank to the floor in numbed shock as Luc walked past her and down the corridor to the lodge.

As the echo of his footsteps faded away, her thoughts spun in ever-decreasing circles in the face of his threats.

She remembered it all. The beauty of her wedding day, the excitement she'd felt that she was finally Mrs. Luc Tanner, then the awful sense of displacement when her father had taken her to one side at the reception:

"I'm so happy to see this has turned out to be a love match after all," Baxter Wallace said.

Belinda's joy in her day dimmed slightly at her father's words. Turned out to be a love match? Hadn't it been that all along?

"What do you mean, Dad? Of course we're in love."

Her father coloured up, blustered through his next few words. *"Luc Tanner has been after you for years, my dear. He made no bones about how he coveted your skills and the way you complemented everything that Wallace Hotels encompasses. I always stood in his way, but now I've seen you two together, so happy together, I don't feel so bad about it all anymore."*

"Bad about what?" Belinda persisted.

"Oh, just men's business. Nothing you need to worry your pretty head about, my dear. Suffice it to say your mother and I are very happy."

Her father's patronising manner set her teeth on edge. This was precisely what had held her back in her endeavours to break free of his expectations all her adult life.

"Tell me," she demanded, meeting her father's worried glance with a firm determination that left him in no doubt that she wasn't going to let the matter go.

"Well, you know how we were hit with that international credit-card-booking scam, how we were out to the tune of several hundred thousands of dollars."

"Yes, but I thought you said you'd sorted that out with the bank."

"Well, yes, I did. But with your mother's ill health and with waiting to get booked into that special treatment in the States, we needed a little more."

"A little? How much, Dad?"

"Luc Tanner loaned us the money to get out of trouble."

"So you set up a loan. Why do you need to feel bad about that?" she asked, confused. It wasn't unusual for this sort of thing, surely.

"Not exactly a loan. Tanner had specific conditions. Actually, one specific condition."

Belinda's heart clenched at her father's words. She knew what he was going to say before he even said it.

"He wanted you. As his wife."

"He bought me?"

How could it be true? Had her father really traded her to offset his debts?

All her life her father had treated her like something to be shown off. Even her showcase gardens had been boastfully spoken of, although he'd never really believed it was more than a hobby for her. He'd paraded her at his side with what she'd hoped was parental pride. But she'd been wrong—terribly, horribly wrong. She'd been nothing more than a chattel in her father's household to be sold to the highest bidder. To another man who regarded her as little more than another acquisition.

"You exaggerate, my dear. You always did.

Always so romantic and emotional about things. Besides, it's not as if you're not in love with him, is it? You'll be very happy together—a perfect couple. You'll be such an asset to his business, just the thing to counter any lingering doubts people have about his background. And the best thing is that now your mother can have the treatment her doctor has been recommending in the States. As soon as she's well enough to travel we can be on our way."

Her father's words fell on her like hail stones, each one a stinging strike against her heart. She didn't want to believe it was true, that she'd been sold to the highest bidder. There was only one person who could refute her father's ridiculous claims.

Luc. Only he could tell her the truth. Of course they'd married for love.

Luc appeared at her side in sartorial splendor, his tailored tuxedo giving him an even more powerful presence than usual.

"*Are you almost ready to leave? The valet has brought the car around.*"

Belinda placed a shaking hand on his arm.

"*Is it true? Did you buy me?*"

"*Buy you? Where did you get that idea?*"

Luc shot Baxter Wallace a damning look, but it was all Belinda needed to know the truth.

"*Luc, tell me you love me. Tell me you married me because you love me.*"

"*Belinda, this is ridiculous. We're married. Come, the car is waiting.*"

She shook free of his grasp. "*Tell me you love me.*" *She enunciated each word carefully so there could be no doubt.* "*Tell me you didn't just marry me to have a hostess at Tautara Lodge.*"

"*Of course I didn't marry you just to have a hostess at Tautara. I could have employed any one of my competitors' best staff for that role, if that was all I wanted.*" *He lifted a finger to stroke the line of her collarbone, exposed by the scooped décolletage of her wedding gown.*

Despite the way her world had tilted off its axis, the action sent a shiver of longing, of promise, through her body. "You know we have more, much more than that."

"So you have no objection to me continuing to develop my career in landscape design? Or the television program I'm supposed to start in a few months?" she probed, knowing before he spoke what his answer would be.

"You won't have time for that. You'll be too busy. With me. With the lodge."

Her blood turned to ice in her veins at his words. She truly was no more than an acquisition to him. A perfect complement to the perfect world he'd created. A world that was in high demand with the rich and famous, a world that was envied by those who lacked the resources to provide the luxurious amenities Tautara Lodge boasted. A world in which she was nothing more than a prized possession.

She was a thing. Not a partner.

A lover. Not beloved.

"I can't do it." The words tore from her throat on a sob as all her dreams for the future crumbled into dust. She gathered her skirts in her hands and pushed past the two men. "It's over. I can't do it. I can't be married to you."

Her father and Luc stood, frozen, as she all but ran for the side entrance of the crowded ballroom at the lakeside hotel where their wedding had been hailed as the event of the year. Wrapped in the celebrations and the dancing, no one saw her leave the room. She moved as quickly as she could down the corridor to the hotel lobby and then out the front doors to where Luc's gleaming black Porsche Carrera GT stood idling on the fore-court.

She flew around the side of the car to the open driver's door, shoving the voluminous clouds of her gown around her legs as she placed her feet on the pedals. She pulled the door shut and crunched the car into first gear, her foot already pressing down on the accelerator.

Then, out of nowhere, Luc loomed dark and large in front of the car. She pushed her foot down hard on the brake but the slippery soles of her new wedding shoes slid sideways, onto the accelerator. She screamed as the car lurched forward, as she heard the sickening crunch—as she struck the man she loved with every shard of her broken heart, and his body rolled across the hood of the car before falling to the gravelled drive.

Horrified, she wrested the steering wheel to the right, away from Luc's falling form, desperately trying to shift her foot from the accelerator to the brake. But her heel caught in the folds of her gown and the last thing she saw before impact was the solid concrete block wall in front of her.

The numbed shock with which she'd recalled their wedding night soon receded, leaving a throbbing, dull ache in the region of her heart and a nauseating pitch in her stomach. How could she have been so easily duped? All her life she'd believed she would only ever marry for love. And she had. She had loved Luc with every part of her—mind, body and soul. Still did and that was more than half the problem.

That was why she now felt doubly betrayed, not just by his admission that he had never loved her, on the night of the wedding, but by his unemotional determination that their lives should still carry on as they had before. That her discovery of the truth should have no bearing on his grand plan for his world.

She staggered to her feet and closed the door, letting it slam hollowly behind her as she collapsed into one of the large leather couches and curled herself up into a ball of hurt. She remembered it all now. The first time she'd seen Luc, the first time he'd spoken to her. The night he'd asked her to marry him. Every memory was bittersweet, overshadowed by the knowledge that for him she'd been a project. Something to be attained.

No wonder she'd reacted so vehemently at the hospital, and no wonder her father had been so uncomfortable. These past days she'd been living the wrong life.

She'd been betrayed at every turn. By her husband. By her father. And now she was trapped in this castle of her husband's self-made kingdom. There was no way she could walk out now, not with her mother's life in the balance. If it had simply been a matter of her father's losses she was sure she could have done it— walked away from Luc to an uncertain future— but as things stood, she couldn't destroy what chance her mother had at being well again.

She imagined her sisters would tell her to get her act together, to be thankful for the fact she had a wealthy husband and an enviable life-style. Things that they'd deemed far more necessary than love. Yet they'd found love with their life partners and their growing families. They were fulfilled.

Family. A shudder ran through Belinda's body. Just prior to their marriage Luc had said he wanted to start a family immediately. She'd pouted and said she wanted him to herself a while before they started trying, and had explained about the long-term birth control she used, something that wasn't subject to the vagaries of time zones in different countries, forgetfulness or illness. So long as she had her shot every twelve weeks she was fine. They'd agreed she'd have one dose prior to the wedding and that they'd review their desire for a family afterward. Now she could only be thankful that there was no way she could be pregnant.

Did she really want to subject a child to a loveless parent? Would that be fair to any of them? The imbalance between herself and Luc would wreak its own toll.

Out of loyalty and responsibility to her family she might not be able to leave Luc, but she could make certain that he wouldn't be able to build his dynasty and inflict on any child the kind of loveless expectations he'd imposed on her.

She dragged in a breath and filled her lungs, wishing she could fill herself with purpose as easily. She was forced to accede to Luc's wishes. To be at his side, to welcome his guests, to ensure that his world was as smoothly run as he deemed necessary. He'd have his perfect bride—the hostess guests from the world over would talk about long after they'd left Tautara Estate. And that was where it began and ended.

Belinda unfolded her legs from underneath her and rose to her feet, her limbs a little unsteady as she walked toward the phone to make the call that would end the beginning of her dreams. By the time she hung up from talking to Jane Sinclair her eyes stung with unshed tears and her throat ached with the words she could never say.

* * *

Luc paced the confines of his office. He hadn't wanted to resort to blackmail but he'd been forced to, to keep Belinda where he needed her. Where he'd always wanted her. Where she belonged.

An image of her as he'd left her a few hours ago burned in the back of his mind. He'd caused her immeasurable pain. He understood that. It was all the more reason not to give rein to that abomination people called love. With love came weakness. Luc Tanner was not weak. He'd clawed his way through life in spite of, or because of, his upbringing.

He rubbed absently at his left forearm, the arm his father had broken the night he'd lost complete and utter control. Max Tanner had been a brutal man, who'd ruled his house with alcohol-fuelled fury. That particular night he'd been more angry than usual, with an edge to his drunkenness that was terrifying. Luc could still hear his mother, more than mildly intoxicated herself, goading Max. He still experienced the bitter taste of fear on his tongue, the absolute helplessness that came from knowing what would come next without being able to do a thing to stop it.

When Max had laid into her with fists and boots, Luc, a lanky twelve-year-old yet to grow into his large hands and feet, had tried to intercede. His father had flung Luc aside, breaking his arm. Then he had gathered his injured wife in his arms, sobbing and professing his undying love to her as he'd carried her out to the car to take her to the emergency room. But his judgment had been too impaired and he'd lost control of their vehicle, killing them both. It had taken several hours before the police had come to find Luc. By then he'd convinced himself he'd heard enough of love.

Locking his emotions away had never been a problem after that. Until he saw Belinda and wanted her with a drive that had superseded even his desire to become a success. So he'd acquired her, much as he would a property from a reluctant vendor. And that was that. That was all there was to it. All there ever would be. All he could allow.

They would make a good life together once she accepted all the benefits she would reap. It might take some time to shore up the wall that had crumbled when her memory had returned, but he was a patient man.

Yet he wanted more. He wanted back the woman who'd opened her heart to him as welcomingly as she'd opened her body. He'd come to relish, indeed look forward to, the sudden lift in his spirits when she was near—the sense of rightness in being together. In being man and wife.

Luc ceased pacing and looked out the floor-length window, over the herb garden she'd lovingly created. He could still see her in his mind's eye as she'd directed his garden staff to lay the pavers in the Celtic knot design, could still see her look up here with a smile upon her face, to his office, where she knew he'd be watching her.

She was an obsession with him. Had been from the first moment. He thought that he could have her, hold her, make love to her, yet still remain aloof—his emotions impenetrable.

And he'd succeeded. Until now.

With a curse Luc strode to his door and flung it open, ignoring Manu's query as he stalked past him, through the main section of the lodge and back toward the suite.

The woman who stood up to greet him as he burst through the door was, to all intents and purposes, the same woman he'd left a few hours ago. He let go of the breath he hadn't realised he'd held trapped in his chest, let go of the fear that she would call him on his threat and have already packed and left Tautara.

She'd changed since their earlier altercation.

Gone was the casual wear. Instead she wore a sleeveless black dress that crossed over at the front, hugging her perfectly formed breasts like a lover's hands. Blood pooled in his groin. Her feet were showcased in fine strappy heels, and his mind filled with an image of her wearing the absurdly feminine shoes and nothing else. She was perfectly groomed, exquisitely beautiful with not so much as a hair out of place. She was everything he wanted her to be, yet it was as if he beheld a shell of the woman he'd married. And he wanted more than a trophy.

"Finished for the day?" she inquired coolly.

"Yes." He bit the word out. He was finished with the office, at least. The enigma that stood in front of him, that was something else.

"May I pour you a drink?"

"Thanks." Luc shed his jacket and dropped it on the chair beside him.

He watched as she went across the sunken lounge to the minibar built into the corner and deftly removed the foil and cork of a bottle of champagne. Champagne? He'd have laid odds she'd have poured him something else, something raw and burning and on the rocks. She poured two glasses and brought one over to him, clinking their glasses together.

"To our new beginning," she toasted.

Luc eyed her carefully. There was no sign of sarcasm or anger. In fact, her face was completely expressionless.

"Our new beginning." He heaved a quiet sigh of relief and took a sip of his wine. "I'm glad you decided to stay."

"You didn't give me any other option." She settled herself on the leather sofa and crossed one leg elegantly over the other, the fabric of her dress sliding along the length of her thigh to expose her smooth skin. "But you'll be pleased to know I've been thinking these past few hours, and you're right. Love is for fools. You don't need to worry about me—" she hesitated, as if searching for exactly the right word "—compli-cating matters between us."

Who was this woman? What had he done? Had he driven the brightness out of her forever? He sat down next to her, tracing one finger across the top of her knee and along the smooth length of her thigh. He saw the flame of desire light her eyes. Slowly she set her glass down on the coffee table beside her, then placed one hand on his chest, pushing him back against the chair while her fingers deftly unbuttoned his shirt before travelling lower, down across his belly to unfasten his belt.

"You want the perfect wife," she whispered against his lips as she slid onto the floor, kneeling between his thighs and reaching out to push his shirt down off his shoulders, tugging it free of his arms before she unzipped the fly on his trousers. "I can do that."

He groaned as she freed his straining erection and fondled him, her fingers sliding lightly along his shaft before tracing his tip. He wanted this, wanted her. That hadn't changed. And yet she had, and somehow it felt wrong—as if a vital piece was missing.

She reached for her glass, taking a mouthful of champagne then bent forward and took him into her mouth. The contrast between her heated lips and the chilled champagne was sheer torture.

And in the split second before his climax robbed him of all cognitive thought, he couldn't help feeling he'd lost something infinitely precious before he'd even realised it had been his all along.

Thirteen

Luc watched as Belinda took a group of their current guests for a horse trek, their single file leaving the stables and heading into the designated track for beginner riders.

She did this as well as she did everything—a consummate rider, a consummate wife—and he couldn't have asked for more. By day she helped ensure their guests, currently a European prince and his family, make the most of the facilities offered at Tautara. By night she stood at his side as they entertained either formally or informally. Repeat bookings had never been higher. Yet still, he was unsatisfied.

Seeing her interact with the prince's children had been an eye-opener and had reminded him of their discussions about children of their own prior to their wedding. After seeing their youngest guest fall asleep in Belinda's arms yet again last night, he was all the more determined for them to start a family of their own. The picture they made was exquisitely beautiful. The child's face relaxed and reposed, totally trusting, and Belinda's wearing a poignant serenity that showed yet another facet to her capabilities.

Maybe that's what was wrong with him these days, he decided as he turned and went back into the house. That sense of being unsettled, as if something was left undone, unfinished. Perhaps a child would cement things for him now. Take away this emptiness he felt, despite having what he wanted.

Most men would have been happy to have

what he had, would walk over broken glass to have a wife such as Belinda. A wife who each day made certain everything ran as smoothly as possible and that each night filled their moments before sleep with a fiery passion that left him lying limp and sated, drifting into sleep with a sense of completion he'd rarely known in his life. And still something was missing.

He resolved to talk to Belinda as soon as their obligations to their current group were over. Tonight they were taking their guests into Taupo for a lakeside meal, the restaurant having been booked for them solely to avoid threats to personal security or media intrusion. In the morning they would leave. The next group weren't expected until the following weekend. For the next few days, for first time since the day Belinda had recovered her memory, they would be alone at the lodge.

It was the perfect time and opportunity to bring up the subject of children. He smiled.

Their child would be brought into the world as a much-wanted member of his family. He had everything to offer and the resources to guarantee their child lacked for nothing.

The difference between what their child would have and what his own childhood had lacked was gargantuan. Luc's son or daughter would want for nothing and would never have to suffer the pain of two parents who lived their lives to the exclusion of all that was decent and right in a child's world.

With a family of his own he would finally attain every goal he'd painstakingly designed as a way of getting back at his father's influence, of proving he was capable of creating and holding on to his own world. He'd amounted to more than his father had ever dreamed was possible, and every tiny speck of it was his, all his. And there was still so much more he could build on. No matter how difficult his background had been, no matter how painful his childhood, he'd made it. He had it all.

* * *

Belinda looked at her reflection in the bathroom mirror and sighed. The strain of living a lie was beginning to show. She could see it in the fine tracery of lines that were evident around her eyes. She hadn't believed it could be so hard to live as she'd always lived. Doing everything she had to, to the very best of her ability—and her ability and experience were vast. Even Manu deferred to her now when it came to planning their guests' menus and activities during their stay at Tautara. Day by day she'd assumed more responsibility, leaving Manu to focus on the heli-fishing, rafting and guided fishing trips, and Luc to do, well, whatever the hell Luc wanted to do.

She gripped the cool marble of the vanity until her fingers ached as she tried to force down the anger she felt every second she thought of her husband and his manipulation of her life.

And the worst of it was she let him.

But it had to be worth it, she consoled herself.

She'd heard from her parents that her mother's treatment in the States was proving to be a major success, she was responding to the drugs and therapies far better than anyone had hoped and could look forward to a long and healthy future. That was what it was all about, Belinda told herself. That her mother be well again. That this—every painstaking day, every heartbreaking night—was worth it. She'd had no idea it would be so damnably hard.

In the bedroom she heard Luc shifting around. Her body betrayingly leaped to life as she reacted to his nearness. He'd been extremely attentive this evening. Under different circumstances she would have relaxed and enjoyed his consideration, but she knew without a shadow of a doubt that Luc Tanner didn't do anything in his world without an ulterior motive.

She'd wondered frequently, in the past few weeks, what had made him that way, and, despite the fact Manu had let slip that they'd been boys together, she could get no further information about what had carved her husband into the granite-hard man he was today.

She straightened up and stiffened her spine, the folds of her nightgown falling gently around her body, skimming her breasts and hips like a soft summer breeze. She drew in a deep breath and walked through to the bedroom.

Luc looked up as she entered, a small frown drawing his eyebrows together.

"Tired?" he asked.

"A little, it's been pretty full-on."

"And you've taken on far more than I had a right to expect. I think it's better if you slow down. Delegate back to Manu more."

He stepped forward and cupped her cheek with his palm. She wished, more than anything, that she could rest her head against the dry heat of his skin and take some comfort from him, but she knew that was impossible. Luc had made it clear he didn't do emotion, he didn't do love, and without either of those she wouldn't accept his consolation, either.

The prospect of the next few years stretched out before her like an arid desert.

"I'll be okay. I like to be busy," she attempted to reassure him.

She turned away from his touch catching, as she did so, the look of irritation that crossed his features. So she'd annoyed him. Right now she didn't care and focused instead on turning down the bed and climbing between the crisp cotton sheets.

The evenings were beginning to get cooler with the onset of autumn. As a gardener she knew autumn shouldn't be her favourite season, but there was something about the change of seasons, the hint of slumber coming with winter's inevitable approach, that she'd always loved.

The valley below them was already turning on an amazing colour display of reds through to golds. She should be thinking about bulb plantings for the spring, she reminded herself, and made a mental note to let the grounds staff know where she wanted them. Of course, in an ideal world she'd have been doing the planting herself. Deciding where to set the displays of tulips and irises she'd loved since she was a little girl. But she'd learned it was easier to delegate those tasks than allow herself to be immersed in her love of the garden again.

It had been easier to give herself some distance from all the things she loved best. It would hurt too much to have to let them go again.

She reached over and flipped off her bedside lamp and settled against her pillows, closing her eyes. When Luc reached for her, as he did most nights, she turned and flowed into his arms. At least physical release guaranteed she would sleep. It was better than lying next to him all night and reliving all those moments when she should have seen the warning signs. The signs that should have told her she'd been reaching for a chimera when she'd agreed to marry him. This was her cross to bear and hers alone.

Even as Luc drew her to him he sensed the emptiness inside her. It echoed in his heart like a hollow shout in a vacant room. She always welcomed their lovemaking each night, but every time he felt as if she drew away from him a bit more. And he hated it. He wanted her back. All of her. Heart and soul.

Tonight he took his time to arouse her, to make sure her body was as hungry for him as he always was for hers. Tonight he wanted to touch her heart, to draw her back to him, the way they'd been before—when she'd loved him.

When he shifted above her and positioned himself at her entrance she was already on the brink of climax, lost in the rhythms, the touches and tastes of their lovemaking. As he eased into her, her fingers clutched at his shoulders and he welcomed the contact. The knowledge that he could bring her to this peak, hold her on the brink of exquisite satisfaction and then drive her over the edge into shattering pleasure was a sharp contrast to the remoteness of their relationship.

Moonlight slanted across the bed. His eyes bored into hers as she felt the tension rise within her, felt her body crest that final wave as he rocked against her. And then, as her body shuddered in release, her eyes squeezed closed and she turned her head on the pillow as if she couldn't bear to acknowledge it was him who had brought her to completion.

He stilled, even as her body continued to pulse around him. He might have her physically, but mentally she was irrevocably lost to him. His heart thudded painfully in his chest and his body cried out in protest as he withdrew from hers unfulfilled. He pressed a hot, damp kiss in the hollow of her neck where it met the curve of her shoulders. Beneath his lips a tremor ran through her, but it gave him no pleasure.

He rolled away from her, and even though no more than six inches separated them on the bed, he felt as if a gulf lay between them. As her breathing slowed and she settled into sleep, he rose from the bed, threw on a robe and left the room.

The next morning Belinda made ready to travel to Taupo Airport in the chopper, where their guests would be met by a private jet to take them on their first leg back home again. It was time for her next injection, and she wasn't prepared to take any risks about bringing a child into what was already a dysfunctional relationship, no matter how long she was tied into it herself.

As she swung her bag over her shoulder and went to leave the suite, Luc came through the front door.

"Manu tells me you're going into Taupo."

"Yes. There are some things I need to take care of."

"What sort of things?"

"Some shopping, things like that." She wasn't about to tell Luc about her appointment to see a local doctor. She had no doubt he'd insist she cancel.

"I need you here today."

Belinda sighed. "Luc, I'll be back by lunchtime, really."

"I'll let Jeremy know he'll be one passenger light. We have things to discuss." He reached for the phone clipped to his belt.

Belinda chewed the inside of her mouth. How much should she tell him? "I have an appointment that I really don't want to change. If I forgo the shopping I can be home again in two hours."

Luc's hand stilled as he punched in the pilot's number and he lifted his head, his eyes boring through her.

"An appointment? What type of appointment?"

"A doctor's appointment, actually." She tried to laugh, to make light of the situation.

"You're having headaches again? Why

didn't you tell me? You shouldn't be seeing a doctor here. We need to see your neurologist in Auckland."

"No, no. It's nothing as serious as that. Look, it's just a simple checkup. Woman's stuff."

"Woman's stuff," he repeated, his voice a monotone. "Contraception, you mean."

"Yes, well, it's time for my shot again. I know we discussed this before we married and we agreed that when the three months were up we'd start to try for a family, but under the circumstances…" Her voice trailed away.

"Circumstances. Would you care to elaborate on that?"

"Luc, really, is this necessary? Of course we can't even think about having a family. A baby needs a loving home, two parents who love each other. We both know that's not the case here. It would be cruel to have a child." *To all of us,* she added silently. "Besides, I really don't think that now is the time to talk about it. Jeremy's waiting."

Luc said nothing, but lifted his phone again and punched in the numbers. "Jeremy? Mrs Tanner won't be travelling with you today. No, that's right. You can head off whenever you're ready."

"What are you doing?" Belinda demanded. "I have an appointment."

"Which you are not going to make. We are going to discuss this right now."

"There's nothing to discuss. I'm not having your baby. It would be monstrous to even think I would do so."

"Sit down, please."

"I'd rather stand, thank you."

Luc stepped closer to her, taking her by the shoulders. The heat of his fingers as they wrapped around her in direct contrast to the pained chill that held her body captive, captive as she was to his need for her as his wife. He gently pushed her down on the sofa behind her and sat down opposite her. She sat stiffly, her shoulders hunched, her hands bunched in fists in her lap.

"I'm not having your baby. That's final. If you won't let me attend my appointment then I'll just sleep elsewhere, the potting shed if I have to."

Luc's sharp bark of laughter lacked any form of humor.

"You will remain in our room, in our bed."

"You can't make me."

"No, I can't make you, any more than I made you stay. I gave you a choice, remember?"

"A choice? You call holding my mother's health, my father's financial security, the jobs of my entire family hostage, a choice? You bullied me into staying and you know it. If you had tied me down you couldn't have been more effective. What on earth makes you think that I would have your child?

"I don't know who or what made you the way you are, Luc Tanner, but you are not the man I thought I fell in love with. You don't have a single compassionate bone in your body. What makes you think you're cut out to be a parent?

How do you expect to raise a child without love? And without that, who's to say it wouldn't turn out to be monster like you?"

Luc stiffened, as if she'd struck him a physical blow. "A monster, you say?"

"You heard me. I made you a promise, that I would stay here, I'd be your wife, I'd be your hostess. That's where it begins and ends. You have no right to demand any more of me and, quite honestly, Luc, I have nothing else left to give you."

Luc watched as she rose and walked gracefully to the bedroom. The "snick" of the door closing echoed emptily through the suite, leaving him alone. Isolated. He replayed her words over and over in his head. *Hostage. Bullied. Monster.* Each one making him no different from the man he hated beyond anything else in the world. Each one transferable to the man he'd sworn he'd be better than.

Each one painfully true.

In the distance he heard the helicopter taking

off and heading out over the valley, toward Taupo. To where Belinda had planned to ensure that they would not have a child. A clawlike grip twisted his insides.

How could he have gotten it all so wrong?

It was simple. He had a life plan and he'd stuck to it, every damn step of the way.

Out on the deck he caught a glimpse of his wife, changed into jeans and a T-shirt, as she shot down the stairs toward the garden. Her sanctuary. A shaft of jealousy burned through him that she'd rather face a pile of dirt and manure than be at his side. A short, sharp expletive expelled from his lips.

He was pathetic. She was right. He was nothing but a bully. In forcing her to stay away from her beloved gardens he'd even denied her the simple pleasure that working in there had brought her, not to mention her shot at the television show. He could see now why it had been so important to her—why she'd wanted so desperately to establish her own independence, her own niche. And he'd done his best to suffocate that precious part of her.

His father had been no different. One by one he'd driven away all his mother's friends. Bit by bit he'd undermined her security until she was totally dependent on him, even so far as to what she wore each day and where she went. It had been her one drunken burst of defiance that had signed her death warrant.

Luc drew in a deep breath. He might not be as physically brutal as his father had been, but psychologically he was no different. Was he so insecure that he couldn't even share her with a group of plants? How on earth had he thought to share her with a child?

His insides twisted even tighter, harder. He dropped his head in his hands and groaned.

No wonder Belinda didn't want to bear his child. In fact, how on earth did she bear his touch? By her own admission she would never give him her heart again. He'd taken the gift she'd given him and he'd thrown it back in her face. Not just once, but twice. Life had given him a second chance when she'd lost her memory. He'd had every opportunity to take that chance, to woo her back, to possibly even learn to love himself. But he'd been so hell-bent on what he'd thought he wanted, he'd wasted that window in time.

The solid realisation of what he'd lost settled like a leaden cloak about his shoulders. How could he have been so stupid? He'd had it all and he'd killed it. Had crushed the life out of any chance their marriage had had, of any chance for him to fulfill his dreams—even reach beyond his dreams—and to believe he could be loved and love in return.

There was only one thing left for him to do to fix this, as much as it killed him inside to do it. He had to let her go.

Fourteen

When Belinda finally came in from the garden, she looked shattered. He knew she'd been working all day, stopping only when he'd insisted Manu take her out a tray with cool drinks and something to eat. Looking at her now made him certain his decision had been the right one.

He, too, had been working hard, on the phone and the Internet, wheeling and dealing. Setting his new future in place.

She didn't even speak to him as she walked past and headed for the bedroom. He followed and watched in silence as she grabbed some clothes from the wardrobe before going into the bathroom.

She stopped in the doorway and turned. "What? Why are you watching me like that?"

"Nothing. I'd like to talk with you when you've had your shower."

"I have nothing to say to you, Luc."

"I know. But I have a lot to say to you, so please, when you're done meet me in my office."

Belinda hesitated a moment. Please? He'd said please? In all the time she'd known him she'd never heard him ask. It was his way to demand, to dictate.

"Belinda?" he prompted.

"Yes, all right. I'll be along shortly."

She shut the door behind her and leaned against it. All she really wanted was to crawl into bed and use sleep to escape the reality that had become her world.

She took her time in the shower, letting the water run over her in streaming jets, washing away the grime of the day. Heading off to the garden as she had, had been a frustrated point of retaliation—a strike back at Luc's draconian attitude. She was paying for it now, she realised, as every muscle in her body ached. But it had been worth it. For a while she'd been able to forget.

By the time she headed back through the main house to Luc's office it was nearly an hour since he'd left her. No doubt he'd be steamed about that, but, Belinda decided with a faint shrug of her shoulders, he'd just have to put up with it.

She'd eschewed the clothing she'd taken from the wardrobe before, instead choosing to dress in a black turtle-neck silk sweater and matching trousers. The fabric whispered across her skin, an imitation of the skim of Luc's touch when he made love to her.

Sex. She corrected herself silently. It was sex, not love. And despite everything, her body still went on full alert at the prospect of being in close proximity with him again. Well, if she had to make the best of a bad thing, at least they had that, she thought cynically. A lot of relationships had less. What kind of person did that make her? She wasn't so sure anymore that she wanted to know.

She knocked once, sharply, on his door and entered his office. Luc rose from behind his desk. He looked pale—the scar on his jawline more prominent than usual, his limp more pronounced as he walked over to the bar installed against one wall to pour two glasses of wine.

"Here, I think we both need this," he said enigmatically.

Belinda took the proffered glass, ignoring the sizzle of electricity that buzzed across her fingers as they brushed against his.

Luc suggested they sit down in the deep leather wing chairs he had positioned near the window overlooking the herb garden. She shot him a surreptitious look as she took a sip of her sauvignon blanc. If anything, he'd grown even paler and his skin appeared to be stretched tightly across his cheekbones and jaw. To her surprise he remained silent.

"So what did you want to discuss, Luc? Our next group of guests?" she prompted, gathering up her nerve for her next comment. "Or perhaps you'd like to browbeat me into bearing your child?"

Luc flinched and pushed himself up from his seat, going to stand at the window, his back to her. When he spoke his voice was low and even, but she could see the tension that bound every line in his body from the way his hand gripped the top of his cane through to the set of his shoulders.

"Neither of those," he eventually replied. "I'm letting you go."

"Go?" Belinda was confused. Did he mean go to a new doctor's appointment or leave Tautara completely?

"Yes. I've arranged for Jeremy to take you to

Auckland as soon as we've finished this discussion. A car will take you directly to your parents' house. Their housekeeper is expecting you."

"But what about the money, what about the debt my father owes you?" Panic flooded her. In light of what Luc had told her about her mother's condition and her treatment, they couldn't afford to stop now any more than her father would be able to drum up the funds necessary to repay Luc at such short notice.

He crossed over to his desk and lifted a sheaf of papers bound by a clip. He handed them to her. "Here's the legal stuff. I know it's only in copy for now, but two originals will be couriered to your parents' house for your attention tomorrow. You'll need to get your own lawyer to look them over. Make any changes you want. I won't contest anything. I'll sign whatever you agree to."

Belinda skimmed the document; her blood turned to ice as she identified a separation agreement. Her fingers rifled through the pages, halting at the page that included in her schedule of personal chattels the debt her father had owed Luc. Her eyes widened as she read the actual sum Luc had bailed her father out for.

"But this is an enormous sum of money. You can't afford to simply write it off," she protested.

"Believe me, I can." Luc sank back into the chair opposite her and picked up his wineglass, swirling the pale-gold liquid around the bowl of the glass. "It was never about the money. It was only ever about you. I made a mistake when I thought I could marry you without love. I deceived you, and for that I'm sorry."

Belinda couldn't speak. She gripped her wineglass so tight she feared it might shatter in her fingers, yet she couldn't make herself relinquish the strangling grip.

Luc looked at her again, his eyes now the dull, flat green of the lake on a dismal cloudy day. She felt his gaze as if it was the touch of his fingers as he let his eyes drift over her face, her throat, then back to meet her own eyes, which no doubt reflected her confusion.

"And now it's over." His voice rasped, sounding as if he had an obstruction in his throat. "Manu has packed some of your things—he'll send the rest on. Jeremy is waiting at the helipad."

He stood and took her hand. For a moment she thought he meant to shake it, as if sealing a business deal, but then he lifted it to his lips, pressing a swift kiss against her knuckles before dropping her hand back into her lap.

"Go," he said, and turned back to the window.

Belinda rose on shaking legs and carefully placed her glass on the wine table between the two chairs. Words escaped her. She'd been summarily dismissed, freed to leave. It was what she'd wanted ever since her memory had returned. Without looking back she left the office and walked straight to the front door and out of the lodge toward the helipad, where she could hear the helicopter warming up, ready to take her away from Tautara, away from Luc.

Manu had just finished loading the last of her cases into the luggage compartment of the chopper as she approached. His dark brown eyes were troubled as she hesitated in front of him, unsure of what to say. When he opened his arms and wrapped them around her she welcomed his embrace.

"I'm going to miss you guys," she said woodenly as Manu handed her up into the passenger compartment.

"We'll miss you, too. I never thought he'd let you go, Belinda. He was different with you. More human, you know? He—" Manu broke off and shook his head. "Just don't think of him too harshly, okay? I've known him all my life. Underneath, he's a good man. A strong man. There are just some demons a man can't let go."

"Why wouldn't you tell me about those demons, Manu? It might have made a difference."

"Not my place to tell. I hoped that one day he'd be ready to tell you himself." Manu shrugged hopelessly. "He's stubborn. Always has been—and had to be, to keep on top."

Belinda nodded sadly. There was nothing else she could do. Nothing anyone could do.

As the Eurocopter lifted off the pad and slowly circled over the lodge before descending into the valley to follow the river to the lake, she dropped her head back against the plush headrest of her seat. She realised she still gripped the separation agreement, and let it drop to the floor. Every cell in her body felt as if it had been wrenched from where it belonged, yet she didn't belong there at Tautara anymore. She didn't belong anywhere.

It was still light as the helicopter approached Auckland's Ardmore Airport to the south of the city. As they set down in the designated area, she could see the sleek dark Mercedes and uniformed driver waiting for her off to one side. She should be thrilled to be free. Free to start again. To start the life she'd always wanted to live until she'd derailed her plans and married Luc.

Her hand shook as she unbuckled her seat belt, and she tried to summon a smile as Jeremy opened the door and held out a hand to help her down from the chopper. He walked with her toward the waiting car.

"I'll send your luggage through behind you. Luc said you'd be eager to get home, so there's no need to wait around for us to unload," Jeremy told her as the chauffeur opened the door to the Mercedes and waited to one side for her to get in.

Belinda halted in her tracks. "No."

"No? You'd rather wait while we unload now?" Jeremy sounded confused.

"No. I don't want you to unload. You're going back now aren't you?"

"After refuelling. But Mrs Tanner, are you sure you don't want your things?"

"Oh, I'm sure I want my things. But I want them to come back with me. You're taking me back."

A huge smile broke across Jeremy's face. "Back to Tautara?"

"Back to Luc."

"What do you mean, he's gone?" Belinda demanded, her head reeling at Manu's news when she arrived back at the estate.

"About half an hour after you left he told me he was leaving. He said he needed to get away for awhile, to think. He didn't expect to be back for several days—maybe longer."

"Couldn't you have stopped him?"

Manu just raised an eyebrow in response. Belinda shook her head. No, Manu could no more have stopped Luc doing whatever he wanted to do than he could stop the flow of the river racing through the valley floor below. But several days? Maybe longer?

"Would you like me to bring your things

inside?" Manu stepped forward to take one of her cases.

"No," she replied quietly. "I'd better leave. There's no point in staying anymore. I'm sorry. I shouldn't have come back."

It was clear to her that Luc had no place for her in his life now he'd made his decision to let her leave, and the knowledge scored her heart like a razor-sharp claw. The journey back to Auckland passed painfully fast and this time she made no objections when Jeremy handed her into the limousine and sent her to her parents' home ahead of her luggage. Right now all she wanted to do was crawl into a deep hole and nurse her wounded soul.

Two weeks later she felt no better. Even working in her parents' extensive grounds offered no solace. Daily calls to Manu hadn't elicited any further information as to Luc's whereabouts. In good news, though, she'd received an e-mail from her father saying that her mother's treatment was nearing its end and her long-term prognosis looked very promising. They'd decided, rather than return immediately to New Zealand, that they'd fulfill a few of their dreams and spend some time touring the U.S.A. together, then doing the same through Europe, before heading home. It brought tears to Belinda's eyes to read that her business-oriented father had realised just how important his marriage was to him. That his wife was more than his right hand—she was his heart, as well, and he wanted to spend as much time with her as they possibly could have together.

If only Luc could have found that denominator in their marriage, Belinda thought as she swiped the tears tracking silently down her cheeks. That balance between love and partnership. If only he'd let her into his heart from the beginning.

Suddenly feeling suffocated by the confines of the house, she went outside into the garden. The sun was lower in the sky as it began to set, casting a golden glow over the foliage and the last of the late-flowering blooms For a moment she regretted sending her parents' housekeeper home for the evening. Right now she'd never felt so desperately alone.

The crunch of a footfall on a fallen leaf made her spin around, her heart racing at the thought of an intruder on the property.

Luc!

Luc's chest tightened as he stopped in his tracks, spellbound at the sight of her. A few weeks ago he'd thought he'd never see her again. His eyes drank in her beauty and he ached to draw her into his arms.

She took a step toward him, her hand outstretched, before she let it drop back to her side.

He cleared his throat before speaking. "You came back to Tautara?"

"Yes."

"Why, when I let you go?"

"You never asked me if I wanted to leave."

Hope began to burn deep inside him. She still wanted him?

"I'd have thought that was obvious. You don't love me anymore. You'd refused to have my child. Of course you didn't want to stay."

"Yet I came back. But you were gone. Why, Luc? Tautara is your home, your dream. Why did you leave?"

"I missed you," he said softly.

Belinda stood, utterly shocked. "Why?"

For a while he couldn't answer, refused to answer and give voice to the words that ached to be spoken.

"Luc?"

"I love you. I didn't want to love you. I didn't want to love anyone. I thought it made a person weak. That it only gave others a chance to hurt you, to make you do things you don't want to do." He reached for her hand. "But you've shown me differently. You've shown me that loving someone and allowing yourself to be loved makes you stronger. And I can't imagine my life without you in it. I want to do things the right way this time. That is, if you'll have me."

"You've always had my heart. But you really hurt me. I felt betrayed when you reduced our marriage to a business deal. You and my father, the two men in the whole world I should have been able to trust, manipulated me. And I've asked myself, over and over, how could I still love you when you used me so badly? There are no easy answers in life, Luc. I think that sometimes we just have to accept things the way they are, but it's important to accept them and then to move on. Not to stay mired in the past. During the past few weeks I thought a lot about love, and a lot about forgiveness. They go hand in hand. I can forgive you for what you did, but only if you can let go of whatever made you react that way, because, you see, it wasn't until we landed at Auckland, the day you sent me home, that I knew I couldn't leave you. If I did I'd be leaving the most important part of me behind—you."

"Are you saying, you'll give me another chance?"

"You love me, Luc. I know that deep in my heart. You could never have let me go if you didn't."

"I do love you. I think I've loved you all along. I let the past keep me from accepting my true feelings for you. I'm asking that you give us another chance. Let's start this marriage over again. Fresh. New. The way we should have started it in the first place. For better or worse, I love you. We can make this work. We can build on what we have as long as we have each other. As long as we can trust each other," he said as he took her hand.

"Yes. We can. We will. Oh, Luc, I love you so much."

Luc pulled her to him, where she belonged.

One day he'd share it all with her—his past, his parents, even old Mr. Hensen. But for now the healing had begun, and all thanks to the wondrous human being in his arms.

"I'm only half a man without you. Letting you go was the hardest thing I've ever done in my entire life. I won't make that same mistake again."

And he didn't.

* * * * *

millsandboon.co.uk Community

Join Us!

The Community is the perfect place to meet and chat to kindred spirits who love books and reading as much as you do, but it's also the place to:

- **Get the inside scoop from authors about their latest books**
- **Learn how to write a romance book with advice from our editors**
- **Help us to continue publishing the best in women's fiction**
- **Share your thoughts on the books we publish**
- **Befriend other users**

Forums: Interact with each other as well as authors, editors and a whole host of other users worldwide.

Blogs: Every registered community member has their own blog to tell the world what they're up to and what's on their mind.

Book Challenge: We're aiming to read 5,000 books and have joined forces with The Reading Agency in our inaugural Book Challenge.

Profile Page: Showcase yourself and keep a record of your recent community activity.

Social Networking: We've added buttons at the end of every post to share via digg, Facebook, Google, Yahoo, technorati and de.licio.us.

www.millsandboon.co.uk